In the Heights

In the Heights of Sinai

# In the Heights of Sinai
## A Hugh Bennett Murder Mystery

**R.Y. Adams**

Copyright © 2024 R.Y. Adams
All rights reserved.
**ISBN:** 978-2-38032-288-0

*"We're a detective…"*
*"You're a detective! I am a chef!"*

In the Heights of Sinai

## CONTENTS

PROLOGUE 9

CHAPTER 1: THE SUNRISE INN 12

CHAPTER 2: UNDER THE STARRY SKY 22

CHAPTER 3: HE'S… HE'S DEAD… 34

CHAPTER 4: THE ARCHITECTS 45

CHAPTER 5: *MULUKHIYAH*, CHICKEN, AND RICE 54

CHAPTER 6: FOOTBALL GAME 63

CHAPTER 7: BREAKING NEWS 72

CHAPTER 8: THE TRADITIONAL MARKET 80

CHAPTER 9: HUGH WANTS TO KNOW MORE 93

CHAPTER 10: DETECTIVE SALAH 110

CHAPTER 11: THE TRAVEL AGENCY 122

CHAPTER 12: SINAI AGAIN 133

CHAPTER 13: ONE COLD WINTER 142

CHAPTER 14: YAHIA'S APARTMENT 148

CHAPTER 15: CLEO HOTEL 159

CHAPTER 16: WINDOW VIEW 175

CHAPTER 17: THE MURDERER 183

CHAPTER 18: ETHAN, HUGH, AND … 204

In the Heights of Sinai

## PROLOGUE

December 1st, 1982

A tall, handsome man walked to a secluded edge of Mount Sinai. He felt the usual tranquillity of Saint Catherine city that night, but it was nevertheless quieter than all the other times he had been there. The gravelly sand made his feet uncomfortable, but he did not mind; the calming scent of the night-time air brought endless peacefulness to his body. The wind caressed his curly dark brown hair, and his round eyes were filled with worry. He wrapped himself tightly with his leather jacket to keep his insides warm but lost to the harsh cold wind that stroked his bones; still, it did not matter to him. His worries buried his physical pain. The man's shoulder bag, a genuine leather weathered with scratches, hugged him perfectly; it was a neat compliment to his casual style. His ice-cold hands reached into the bag, neglecting the freezing breeze, not even trembling once.

He reached for a handkerchief-wrapped object; the square

cloth bore three exquisitely knitted butterflies in each corner, framing an untouched white space at its centre.

The man felt his heart quicken as he revealed the object, its beauty beyond words. It shimmered in the dim night, capturing his intense gaze, and flooding him with countless thoughts.

"Why?" he murmured in a husky voice, then put it back carefully inside and walked calmly, reaching the edge of the mountain. Saint Catherine was his favourite place on earth; it was where his heart found peace. He stared at the cold dark space, then closed his eyes for a moment and took a deep breath. A minute later, he opened his eyes and smiled.

*Saint Catherine, I thank you for washing away my worries.* He felt a sudden warmness flood his body, as if Saint Catherine had smiled back.

"And then there's your serenity, the peacefulness that settles over you at dawn. It's in the gentle rustle of your olive trees in the breeze, the distant call to prayer that drifts through the air. You have a way of making me feel at home. To me, you'll forever be more than just a city," the man muttered to himself with a smile, his eyes lingering fondly on the view before him. "Look at me talking to myself like a madman," he added, a touch of amusement colouring his tone as he chuckled softly to himself.

Approaching footsteps disrupted his connection with the moonlit mountain. "I didn't expect your early arrival," the man said.

He turned back to face the person he awaited, erasing the smile born from his thoughts of Saint Catherine.

Suddenly, a swift blow landed on his face, sending him collapsing to the ground, towards the mountain's edge once again. The impact left his mind foggy, his thoughts scattered. Struggling to focus through blurred vision, he cast a sorrowful gaze towards Saint Catherine, bidding his final farewells. Then, a merciless second strike to the back of his head cruelly stole his last breath.

## CHAPTER 1: THE SUNRISE INN

December 11th, 1982 – 8 hours earlier

Ethan Abbott sat quietly in the reception waiting area. The Sunrise Inn was nestled in a somewhat deserted area of the mountain, surrounded by sparse dwellings that dotted the vicinity. The landscape was minimalistic, with only the distant lights of a small market offering limited snacks, hinting at signs of life. The 36-year-old British private investigator retrieved a brochure he had picked up at the Egyptian museum, tucked away in his jacket pocket, and leafed through it for the hundredth time. The tedious drive from Cairo to Saint Catherine was unbearable for Ethan; he strongly believed that the time spent on lengthy journeys should not count towards the tour days recommended by the travel agency.

He tucked the brochure back in his jacket's pocket, finally losing all thoughts of the motion sickness. He watched the tour group as they shuffled into the lobby, a mix of excited chatter and hushed anticipations. The atmosphere carried a sense of collective eagerness, a shared anticipation for the comfort and exploration that awaited each guest in their new temporary abode.

The one-floor traditional Inn radiated comforting yet vibrant simplicity. The wooden beams overhead, embellished with vibrant fabrics, created an atmosphere of earthy charm. The reception space itself boasted handcrafted wooden furniture, adorned with embroidered orange cushions in warm, earthy hues. Sandalwood and jasmine fragrances lingered in the air, emanating from woven reed baskets filled with dried flowers. Soft rugs, woven with traditional Islamic inspired patterns, lined the floors, introducing a touch of warmth to the cool, tiled surfaces beneath. Lanterns, delicately fashioned from glass and metal, hung from the ceilings, casting a soft, golden glow across the cosy space. Ethan observed the intricate details, finding solace in the tranquil surroundings of the inn.

"Cairo's been a rush like no other. The bazaars bursting with life, the non-stop energy—it feels like we're a world away from everything we know," William expressed, settling into the chair next to Ethan. With sleek black hair and welcoming blue eyes, the 46-year-old William exuded a surprising youthfulness that always caught Ethan's eye.

"Tell me about it; it feels just as invigorating as our first visit," Ethan concurred, appreciating the vibrant energy of Cairo. He continued, "And the Egyptian Museum—it's a treasure trove of marvels. The mummies and ancient artefacts were mind-blowing. Did you manage to dig into the details of those hieroglyphics?"

"I gave it a shot! But honestly, I was more caught up wandering through a maze of wonders than cracking ancient codes. And the pyramids—stepping inside was like time travelling. You really should've come in with me; it was something else."

"Easy on me. You know I'm claustrophobic, and I'm still recovering from my motion sickness here. Seeing the pyramid from the outside was enough, especially with the tour guide mentioning the theory that its placement mirrors the belt of the constellation Orion—it did inspire me to acquire more books on Ancient Egypt though."

"But you hardly ever crack open the books you already have," William teased.

"Maybe I should start." Both men laughed.

"I'm sure the local cuisine was the real highlight of your trip," William said, inching the conversation forward.

"Definitely. That falafel joint we stumbled upon? Absolute gold. I could devour their pita sandwiches every day," Ethan, a culinary maestro, expressed with a satisfied grin.

"Didn't the tour guide mention it's called *taamiyya* in Egypt, not falafel?"

"*Taamiyya*, falafel, whatever it is, it's absolutely delicious."

"Make sure you don't leave Egypt without that recipe. I'll be craving those when we're back home," warned his friend.

"Consider it sorted. Everything's documented right here," Ethan assured, retrieving a small recipe book from his jean's back pocket. "I managed to get all the nitty gritty details from the joint owner. Luckily, he didn't mind sharing the recipe with a British tourist he'll likely never encounter again." The two friends shared a robust laugh, their friendship blending seamlessly with the inviting atmosphere of the cosy inn.

"Choosing Egypt as our first stop was a smart move. I'm happy you came on board for this one-year world trip. It's bound to be helpful," remarked William, luxuriating in a stretch.

"No murders, no Hugh. More Ethan… I can't remember the last time my mind felt at peace," responded Ethan, finishing a can of a welcome Coca-Cola from the inn.

Habitually, he crushed the tin can effortlessly with his bare hands. His attire—blue jeans, a white shirt, and a black leather jacket—provided warmth, a rare departure from Ethan's usual style in London where warmer clothes were essential.

"Why pack Hugh's outfit, though?" Ethan queried.

William, sporting a sincere smile, was convinced he made the right choice. However, he refrained from disclosing it, mindful of sparing Ethan's feelings.

"Have you checked in yet, gents?" Out of breath, Mike Hall, a sturdy African American man in his mid-forties, interjected as he eased into a chair beside the two friends.

"Not yet," Ethan responded. "We'll wait until everyone is finished."

"Despite being the sole guests in the inn, the receptionist mentioned there aren't enough rooms. I'll be sharing a room with the boys over there," he gestured towards Jake and Derek, who were finalizing the check-in process. "I suppose everyone will be rooming with their travel companions." He chuckled. Despite his baldness, Mike Hall's innocent visage compensated for the absence of hair.

"You seem to get along quite well," Ethan remarked. "Considering you work together, the three architects from the one and only New York City."

"Yes, Jake never fails to amuse me, and Derek, oh boy, Derek teaches me all about Japanese culture!"

The three men redirected their attention to Jake, whose laughter reverberated through the room—a lively melody that infused energy into the atmosphere. His blond hair flawlessly complemented his blue eyes, and his animated gestures and constant engagement with others painted a vivid scene of social connection.

"Every tour group needs someone like Jake," William remarked.

Derek, in stark contrast, had notable differences. Despite being 28 years old, just two years older than Jake, he appeared younger. His handsome face was partly concealed by oversized square-rimmed glasses, giving him an air of sophistication. His slim, tall build could have easily been mistaken for that of a pop star in Japan. Despite living in the United States, Derek's traditional Japanese characteristics were clear. Ethan had the fewest interactions with Derek among the tourists. Nevertheless, he found immense joy in the company he shared during his holiday—companionship that exceeded his expectations.

"This place is stunning! I'm excited to discover what Saint Catherine has to offer!" The three men shifted their gaze towards Jacqueline Roux, the group's fashion enthusiast, a thirty-one-year-old French woman employed by a newly established newspaper in Marseilles.

Ethan discerned that Jacqueline's style deviated from the conventional image one might have of a writer. Her ashy blonde hair gracefully cascaded over her broad shoulders, harmonizing with the sparkle in her hazel eyes. During their stay in Cairo, there were moments when onlookers mistook Jacqueline for someone in the entertainment industry. Ethan noticed she didn't mind; in fact, she appeared flattered by the comparison.

Jacqueline's companion, her childhood friend, Brigitte Dubois, who shared the same age, joined her. Their spirited laughter, initially irksome to fellow travellers, had transformed into a familiar melody over the two weeks of their journey. Brigitte's style mirrored her friend's, frequently adorned in knee-length dresses complemented by vibrant coats and dark stockings. Her black pencil skirt and grey cable-knit jumper harmonized well with her short, dark brown hair and eyes. Despite attracting less attention than Jacqueline, it wasn't due to any lack of beauty on Brigitte's part.

Ethan found himself captivated not just by Brigitte's physical appearance but also by her unwavering confidence. Unbeknownst to him, it wasn't merely her self-assurance that set her apart; it was her intelligence, vividly reflected in her brilliantly shining eyes. Brigitte, he learned, worked as a tour guide at the esteemed Louvre Museum in Paris.

"This place has more of a traditional vibe. I already miss the luxury of the Cleo Hotel." Ethan chuckled as he compared Saint Catherine city's Sunrise Inn to the Cleo Hotel they lodged in during their time in Cairo.

"Try to appreciate the traditional atmosphere of the Sunrise Inn for a few days. Then, we go back to Cairo's Cleo Hotel before we head home!" Jacqueline said cheerfully.

"I guess I should." Ethan said.

"The street outside is a haven of peace, and I'm in love with that Bedouin seating area. Jaq, imagine us sipping hot chocolate there as the evening settles in!" Brigitte exclaimed to her friend.

"I'm so excited for that," Jacqueline replied, adjusting her short blue dress to ensure it covered her knees.

"Our amazing tour guide, do join us for a moment," Brigitte beckoned as Yahia Taha approached the group gathered in the reception waiting area.

The tour guide's eyes sparkled with appreciation at the compliment, and Ethan couldn't help but notice the two matching leather bags they both carried, proudly displaying the inscription 'Tour Guide and Proud.'

"Everyone, how are you finding the inn?" Yahia inquired, his slightly dark complexion adding a touch of warmth to his welcoming demeanour. His mannerisms exuded amiability, and he appeared proud to ensure the comfort and contentment of his diverse group of tourists.

"Cosy but not enough rooms," Mike responded bluntly.

"Love it!" Brigitte and Jacqueline exclaimed simultaneously, the shared laughter creating a harmonious atmosphere.

"Well, the most challenging part is having to share a room with William," Ethan jestingly remarked.

"Then let's rush the check-in process and overcome this, shall we, Ethan?" William suggested, rising from his seat.

"Sure."

The two men made their way towards the reception area, leaving behind the cosy seating and the lively ambiance of the inn. The reception area directly confronted the entrance, featuring an extended black desk resting gracefully on the tiled floor. Behind it, a chair stood against the wall, showcasing rustic room keys. Corridors housing the hotel rooms flanked the reception on both sides, ending in a study room and seating area.
"We expect more guests to arrive tomorrow. Also, regrettably, the phones are currently out of order, but we are diligently

working on resolving the issue," the teenage receptionist joyfully shared as the two friends checked in.

"Quite all right, thank you," responded William.

"I find it rather odd," remarked Ethan as they awaited the young receptionist to hand over their keys. "Remember our time at Sinai Bird Travel Agency, waiting for our assigned guide? One employee whispering about Yahia's previous aggressiveness and lack of enthusiasm?"

"Ah, yes. I remember that quite well. If it held any truth, Yahia has certainly undergone a transformation. Earning the title of 'employee-of-the-month' doesn't align with what that employee said," replied William.

Yahia interrupted their conversation. "Alright, everyone, huddle up," he announced, bringing his arms together in a sweeping gesture to signal the assembly. "Dinner is scheduled for 7 PM in the outdoors area. Take your time to relax until then."

A sudden thud grabbed the group's attention as something tumbled from Yahia's meticulously-kept bag. The unexpected occurrence startled only two of them profoundly.

## CHAPTER 2: UNDER THE STARRY SKY

The outdoor area of the Sunrise Inn emanated a charming Bedouin style, snuggled under the Egyptian night sky. The cold weather wrapped the gathering in a crisp embrace as they settled on intricately patterned cushions arranged around low wooden tables, with blankets for guests to warm themselves up with. A gentle breeze carried the scent of burning cedar from a nearby bonfire, casting a warm glow over the tourists' faces. The flickering flames danced to an unseen rhythm, creating a mesmerizing display. Dinner was served in traditional Bedouin fashion, with aromatic dishes spread across the tables, inviting everyone to indulge in the rich flavours of Egyptian cuisine. The lively chatter of the group mixed with the crackling of the bonfire created an atmosphere of contentment amidst the chilly desert night.

Jacqueline, with her lively manner, took the lead in the conversation. "Ladies, I must say, it's absolutely delightful that we've all agreed to buy the same charming shawl from

Khan Al Khalili market in Cairo. It's not only pretty but also a steal at that price!"

Brigitte, Daniela, Mrs Hottinger, and Soo Ah exchanged glances before nodding almost simultaneously.

"Just lovely, isn't it? Brown with those striking black tassels," Jacqueline enthused, her eyes shimmering with excitement. "I spotted it and couldn't resist. A unique find. I'm wondering why Brig and I seem to be the only ones flaunting it, though."

"It's a little chilly for me at the moment," Daniela chimed in, drawing laughter from the ladies.

Brigitte, a touch reserved, added, "Yes, it caught my eye, too. The intricate details make it really special."

Daniela nodded in agreement, her eyes reflecting a quiet appreciation for the shawl's craftsmanship.

"Jun Hyuk and I strolled through Khan Al Khalili market. He insisted I choose something beautiful, and I'm glad I settled on the brown shawl after Jacqueline suggested we all buy matching ones." Soo Ah smiled.

"Well, all you ladies look exceptionally elegant with these shawls," Ethan remarked, and the women laughed.

"It seems we all have a penchant for the same exquisite piece. How amusing," Mrs Hottinger, who had observed the interaction silently until then, finally spoke up.

Daniela's eyes fixated on Soo Ah's intricate gold hairpin, the Binyeo, settled delicately in her black hair. A majestic phoenix, its wings outstretched, graces the crest of the Binyeo, its plumage etched with extraordinary detail. The feathers seem to flutter.

Daniela couldn't contain her curiosity any longer. "Soo Ah, that gold hairpin is absolutely stunning. Is it a traditional Korean piece?"

Soo Ah's eyes sparkled with pride as she touched the Binyeo, a familial relic passed down through generations. "Yes, it's a Binyeo, a traditional Korean hairpin. This one has been in my family for decades."

The other ladies leaned in, their interest piqued by the gleaming piece. Mrs Hottinger, with her refined taste, nodded approvingly. "How fascinating! The craftsmanship is remarkable. It must hold sentimental value for you."

Soo Ah nodded, her mind travelling to the past. "It's a connection to my roots, a reminder of the strength and grace that runs in my family."

"The design is so intricate; it's a work of art," Brigitte added.

"When you visit Korea, Daniela, you must let me buy these splendid Binyeos for you," Soo Ah graciously offered.

"Thank you, Soo Ah," Daniela responded with a warm smile.

"In that case, I should consider a trip to Korea as well," Jacqueline quipped, eliciting laughter from the group of ladies.

Mrs Hottinger's shifted towards her brother, a subtle exchange of glances between the two.

"You've had a handful of lamb chops, Nico, slow down a bit. It's not good for your health," nagged Mrs Flavia Hottinger. The forty-year-old Swiss widow was touring Egypt with her brother, Nico, and niece, Daniela.

"Oh, come on, it is a once in a lifetime experience." Mr Hottinger furrowed his brow, reflecting his irritation. He sighed, longing for a moment of peace. The sand beneath his feet seemed to absorb his frustration as he wished for a respite from the ceaseless commentary of his well-meaning but vexing sister. Despite being in his early fifties, his slumped posture and the cane in his right hand made him seem much older.

"Daniela, dear, why aren't you eating?" asked Mrs Hottinger as she shifted her nags to her 18-year-old niece. Daniela sat quietly between her father and aunt, her light brown hair falling gracefully around her shoulders. Dressed in a simple and casual outfit, she wore a thick black jacket that provided comfort against the chilly weather. Her choice of sneakers hinted at a practical, laid-back style.

"I'm not a big fan of lamb..." Daniela said, her green eyes gesturing towards the unfamiliar dishes. She sighed uneasily, scanning the array of food, and observing the other diners before turning her attention to Yahia.

"Mr Taha, is there anything else to eat other than lamb?" However, Yahia seemed preoccupied, lost in his own thoughts.

"Yes, please. My daughter needs to take her medication, and it's not recommended to take on an empty stomach," Mr Hottinger addressed Yahia.

"Oh, it's not necessary to take the medications now, Nico. It's already nice and calm here," Mrs Hottinger said to her brother, then turned her attention to her niece. "Don't you think so, dear? She needs to eat, though. Please ask the chef if there is anything else to serve, Mr Taha."

Despite their plea, Yahia ate slowly and displayed a lack of appetite, as if he hadn't heard her.

"Mr Taha? Mr Taha?" Daniela called twice until she finally caught his attention.

"Oh, Daniela. I'm sorry. Of course," he responded, then summoned the old chef, Chef Fakhri, who hurried over.

"Is there something wrong with the food?" the chef inquired, addressing Yahia.

"No, the food is wonderful," Yahia replied. It's our young one here who isn't used to our traditional fare. If you could prepare something more to her taste, we'd highly appreciate it."

The chef appeared momentarily perplexed before Daniela interjected, "Any sandwiches would be fine." The seasoned chef nodded and excused himself.

"What medications do you take, Daniela?" Jake asked, delicately carving into the lamb.

All three Hottingers exchanged glances.

"It's anxiety medication. Our dear Daniela suffers from minor anxiety, nothing to worry about," Mr Hottinger explained, fixated on his plate.

"Well, Daniela, if you need anything, I used to be a clinical psychologist. I'm here if you ever want to talk," William offered kindly. Daniela shrugged and remained silent.

"So, what prompted you to stop practising psychology and take up private investigation?" asked Jacqueline.

"Yes, that's a big shift. What triggered it?" Derek asked as he smiled warmly at Jacqueline.

"Well, let's say a friend persuaded me to do it," William replied.

"Persuaded *us*!" Ethan said. "You know? I aspired to start my own restaurant business, but again, that same friend talked me out of it and persuaded me into the world of investigation."

"I can't imagine the persuasion skills that friend must have," Mike chuckled. The group laughed in agreement.

Ethan watched the newlywed Korean couple, Jang Jun-Hyuk and Kim Soo-Ah, who were deeply in love, openly holding hands and displaying their affection. Despite their comfort with each other, they remained reserved around the rest of the group.

"Is this a MAVICA camera? A gadget I've wanted for so long. I searched all London stores for it before this trip, but it was sold out everywhere," Ethan asked Jun-Hyuk, who held the camera ready to capture moments during the meal.

"Yes! Perfect for this trip. Here, Ethan, take a look," Jun-Hyuk said, handing the camera over to him. Holding it now, like a child with a new toy, he examined it thoroughly. Ethan's desire for the gadget surged even more.

"Try taking a picture," Jun-Hyuk encouraged.

"Alright, ladies, gather around for a picture," Ethan exclaimed. While Daniela was occupied with the cheese sandwich the chef had prepared for her, Soo-Ah, accompanied by Mrs Hottinger and the French friends, shared a collective smile for the photograph.

"One more photo with everyone gathered." Ethan couldn't hide his excitement, secretly relishing the opportunity to capture more moments with the cool gadget.

The group assembled, and Ethan snapped the picture. The flash illuminated for a second, capturing genuine smiles from everyone.

"Alright. Who's up for authentic Bedouin tea and stargazing by the campfire?" Yahia said, rising from his seat and casually brushing off any sand that had come across his pants.

Under the expansive mountain night sky, the group gathered around the crackling campfire, enveloped by the serene darkness. The stars above twinkled like diamonds strewn across an ebony canvas, creating a celestial spectacle that left them in awe. The heat from the fire danced with the cool mountain breeze, creating a perfect balance. Yahia, their guide, skilfully brewed authentic Bedouin tea, the aroma wafting through the air. The tourists, cups in hand, gazed upward, marvelling at the vastness of the cosmos. Each sip of tea carried a blend of tradition and warmth, echoing the company of the diverse group beneath the celestial expanse. Ethan couldn't help but initiate the conversation.

"Have any of you read about the legends surrounding this mountain?" he asked, his eyes gleaming with anticipation.

Brigitte chimed in with a knowing smile. "Oh, absolutely! The tales of divine revelations and the Burning Bush are enthralling. It's incredible to think that we're standing on such historically rich grounds."

Brigitte, sipping on her tea, continued. "Imagine the ancient pilgrims making their way through these paths. The sense of spirituality must have been overwhelming."

Derek nodded in agreement. "This mountain is massive. Back in the Big Apple, it's all skyscrapers. But here, it's all about nature's grandeur."

As the group continued their discussion, Mike interrupted with a historical titbit. "I heard that the Saint Catherine's Monastery, placed at the foot of the mountain, has been a haven for knowledge seekers for centuries. Its library holds priceless manuscripts dating back to ancient times. It's the one we're seeing tomorrow, right, Yahia?"

Yahia nodded.

The Korean couple exchanged whispers in awe. Jun-Hyuk, with his camera hanging around his neck, captured the essence of the moment. Soo-Ah, fascinated by the rich history, expressed, "Korea is seventy percent mountains but I've never seen a rocky mountain like this one. The magnificence of this mountain is unreal."

Daniela listened intently, absorbing the shared knowledge. Her eyes, the colour of emerald, reflected the starlit sky above. Mrs Hottinger, with her motherly aura, noticed Daniela's interest and gently asked, "What's on your mind, dear?"

Daniela hesitated before speaking softly. "It's just... this place feels ancient, like it holds secrets that've been trapped here for centuries. I wonder what stories the mountain would tell if it could speak."

Yahia couldn't help but smile at their exchange. "The desert's silence, the rugged terrain, and the ancient monastery—they all contribute to an unparalleled experience. It's as if time slows down. You've all captured the essence of Saint Catherine magnificently. Each rock, each whisper of the wind, and every star above has a story to share. You know what? My favourite part is when the cool breeze gently sweeps over the mountain; it's enchanting, like it's safeguarding delightful memories beneath its airy touch."

Under the vast canvas of the Egyptian night sky, with Saint Catherine's Mountain as their backdrop, the group shared a moment of unity and appreciation for the timeless beauty that surrounded them.

Brigitte approached Yahia with a warm smile, her eyes reflecting both curiosity and admiration for the breath-taking surroundings.

"Yahia, what can you share about the local Bedouin culture around Saint Catherine?"

Yahia, however, seemed momentarily preoccupied, his eyes darting towards the towering peaks of the mountain. "Ah, the Bedouin culture is rich and deeply intertwined with the landscape here. They've been the guardians of these sacred lands for generations," he replied, his tone a blend of knowledge and evasion.

Undeterred, Brigitte persisted, sensing a subtle distance in Yahia's demeanour. "I've heard tales of the Bedouins' connection to the mountain, their intimate knowledge of its secrets. Have you had any personal experiences with them?"

Yahia, while maintaining his polite manner, subtly shifted his focus away. "Certainly, I've interacted with many Bedouin guides over the years. Their stories add layers to the mystique of this place. But you know, there's always more to discover."

Brigitte, though perceptive, decided not to press further, respecting Yahia's tacit reluctance to share more personal anecdotes. Instead, she pivoted the conversation back to the group, highlighting the wonder of the surroundings.

"I can't wait to explore the ancient paths leading to the summit tomorrow! The views must be amazing," Brigitte exclaimed, her eyes fixed on the rugged terrain that lay ahead.

Yahia, momentarily drawn back into the group dynamics, nodded in agreement. "Absolutely. The trek to the summit is both challenging and rewarding. It has a unique perspective of the desert landscape and the surrounding peaks."

As the night unfolded, the group continued their animated conversations, each member contributing to the shared experience. The flickering flames of the campfire cast a warm glow, and the stars above seemed to twinkle in approval of the diverse group that had gathered beneath the timeless embrace of Saint Catherine's Mountain.

After the campfire-lit dinner, the six rooms of the Sunrise Inn quickly filled up. Despite Ethan's claim that he wasn't pleased to share a room with William, there was an underlying contentment. As he lay in bed, he contemplated how the Hottingers, known for their frequent arguments, would fare in a single room before succumbing to a deep sleep.

## CHAPTER 3: HE'S... HE'S DEAD...

Ethan awoke a few hours past midnight, the room in the traditional Egyptian inn cloaked in a cool darkness and unfolded with an air of elegance. The floor, cool underfoot, boasted a mosaic of earthy tiles depicting scenes of desert life. Draped in rich, embroidered fabrics, the windows allowed glimpses of the quiet street below. Heavy curtains, adorned with golden tassels, swayed gently in the breeze. The furniture was weathered by years of use, and Ethan's bed, with a carved wooden headboard, dominated one corner, decorated with vibrant blue and yellow textiles. The scent of aged wood and faint traces of incense lingered. Ethan's eyes shifted to the bed beside him, where William Harrington lay, a friend and now, a business partner. Despite the shared room's chill, the heater proved ineffective. An unusual thirst stirred within Ethan, prompting a search for a bottle of water. Ethan

seldom roused from sleep for sustenance. Was it truly Ethan, or someone else within, calling out for water?

With a loud yawn and a stretch of his arms, Ethan's messy, dark brown hair partially covered his sharp eyebrows, matching in colour. His oversized, worn-out pyjamas hung loosely on him. In the barber's mirror, Ethan glimpsed his reflection, feeling a familiar unease. Appearance held little significance to him; his attire was always the shabbiest. Still half-asleep, he rose from bed, muttering, "I never cease to startle myself."

As he made his way towards the door, a sudden scream pierced the air from the seated area, jolting him from his thoughts. The word "dead" echoed in his ears, sending a shiver down his spine. "Dead?... Who's dead?... What's going on…?" Ethan whispered to himself after he had heard bits and pieces of the ruckus outside.

An immediate pounding headache gripped him. Reaching for the cupboard opposite his bed, Ethan struggled to avoid collapsing. Clutching his head tightly, he attempted to alleviate the piercing pain.

Struggling to reach his prescribed pain medications on a low wooden table decorated with delicate brass ornaments between the beds, Ethan's mental anguish caused him to falter, dropping the pills and knocking over the table. William, awoken from his bed, reacted quickly. Though not an unfamiliar situation, it hadn't occurred in quite some time. He retrieved the pills and restored the wooden table, leaving the fallen ornaments behind.

"No, don't!" Ethan screamed, hands tightly gripping his head, eyes shut firmly.

"Here you go," William reassured, placing the pills in Ethan's hand. Despite William's attempts at a composed demeanour, subtle signs painted a picture of someone grappling with inner tension.

Ethan remained unresponsive, a sudden tranquillity enveloping him, dispelling his pain. Slowly turning his head towards William, his eyes still shut, he gradually opened them, gazing intently. Ethan's eyes

appeared altered, deeper, more intense. Surveying the dim room briefly, he then returned his gaze to his friend.

"Dr Harrington, it's been a while."

"Hugh?"

\*\*\*\*\*\*\*

The dimly lit room buzzed with an uneasy energy as Hugh, apparently dissatisfied with his appearance, cast a disdainful glance at himself in the barber's mirror, unhappy with the clothes Ethan had dressed him in. Hugh decided not to change them but managed to fix his hair using styling gel from Ethan's bag. William, extending a gesture of assistance, was met with Hugh's aggressive rebuff, leaving an air of tension lingering between them.

"Somebody's dead," Hugh declared with a sombre tone, his words hanging in the dimly lit space.

William, seeking clarification, pressed, "What are you talking about?" However, Hugh, unperturbed, brushed past him towards the seating area, and William trailed behind nervously.

In the study room and amidst the shadows, Derek appeared breathless and visibly terrified, his dishevelled appearance hinting at the urgency of the situation. Mr Hottinger and his sister huddled around him, forming a concerned circle. Derek, struggling to articulate the troubling news, managed to convey, "The tou... tour... tour guide... he's dead."

"Oh, Ethan, William, you're awake!" Mr Hottinger exclaimed, trying to shift the focus away from the distressing news that Derek had just shared.

In contrast, Mrs Hottinger said, "Poor Derek. We were startled by hurried footsteps, and he burst in, repetitively yelling 'he's dead! He's dead!'" Her gaze briefly diverted to Hugh, acknowledging his well-groomed hair. Hugh couldn't suppress a smirk.

"Hand him some water," William suggested as he motioned to Mrs Hottinger, aiming to provide comfort amid the unfolding chaos. Mrs Hottinger promptly poured a glass of water from the jar stationed on the table beside the couch next to her.

"Where is the body?" Hugh asked.

"Five kilometres north of the hotel.... By the mountain edge...." Derek said out of breath.

Jacqueline, clad in blue pyjamas, entered the seating area; she voiced her sleep troubles in a comical manner. "I couldn't sleep a wink! I'm constipated, sleepless, and need earplugs to block Brigitte's snoring!" she complained, earning a sarcastic glance from Hugh.

Jacqueline, bewildered, inquired, "What's going on?" as she surveyed the surroundings, sensing an undercurrent of tension in the air.

"Let's go," Hugh gestured at William, dismissing Jacqueline's question. The two men put on their coats and made their way towards the mountain.

With a white cloth that he had grabbed on his way out, Hugh meticulously examined the lifeless form of Yahia. The tour guide's left arm lay motionless, adorned with a simple watch that had frozen at 1:10 a.m., a poignant symbol marking the abrupt end of his existence. As Hugh surveyed the scattered contents of Yahia's open leather shoulder bag, he couldn't discern anything of particular interest.

"Wallet, a map of Sinai, and the Sunrise Inn check-in receipt. Pretty clean," William said as he examined what Hugh took out of Yahia's bag. "But the ornament from earlier is missing. Someone must be after it."

"What ornament?"

"Something fell out of his bag while we were checking-in earlier. Didn't have a look at it. It was covered with a white handkerchief."

Hugh, with his seasoned eye, observed the corpse with a mixture of detachment and purpose.

"No visible bruises nor signs of conflict. Only this strike on the face... probably hesitation by the murderer. Then I believe there was a brief pause before the assailant continued with the brutal act," Hugh said confidently. "However, this second strike in the back is full of confidence and brutality; the murderer overcame his initial reluctance."

"Hmm…"

"Someone must've turned the body."

"If the second strike was on the back, then he must have fallen on his face," William agreed.

"The dirt on his face does seems to support that," Hugh concurred.

"Look at this," William gestured to the rocky ground. "No shoe prints. The wind must have wiped them clean."

Hugh scrutinised the terrain surrounding them, a contemplative silence enveloping him as he delved into the recesses of his thoughts; the eerie silence of the mountain surrounded him. A peculiar emotion lingered within him, one that eluded description. It was a sensation familiar to him, resonating whenever a murder transpired. Perhaps it was more personal this time, given the familiarity he felt with the deceased tour guide.

Standing side by side, William and Hugh conveyed an unspoken mourning for the departed soul. The silence endured for a minute or two, as if paying tribute to a fallen comrade. William crouched down on both knees beside Yahia, murmuring a silent prayer—a custom he adopted whenever he encountered a dead body.

"Welcome to Egypt," William broke the silence, attempting to infuse a hint of normalcy into the unsettling atmosphere.

Hugh, donned in Ethan's clothes but with a gaze that betrayed an alternate persona, remained in a stoic silence.

"I packed your clothes, you know," William continued, undeterred by Hugh's lack of response.

William, sensing the weight of the moment, decided to give them more time to mourn the loss of the tour guide.

"You know, Hugh, I can't help but think about how Ethan's life changed since your parents passed away," William finally decided to break the silence for the second time, his voice a subdued murmur in the vast quiet of the mountain. Hugh's eyes flickered with a trace of recognition but remained focused on the scene before them.

"It was a difficult period for Ethan," William continued, selecting his words with precision. "He inherited the restaurant, but its essence changed without his parents. The once bustling establishment, a vessel for memories and the dreams they once shared, became a reminder of what was lost. Still, he wanted to keep it; it was the only thing he had left."

A distant look crossed Hugh's face, a reflection of the turbulent emotions within him.

"But you decided to sell Ethan's restaurant," William observed, his tone empathetic. "Because there was Hugh, the private investigator. A new path."

The mountain cast long shadows, adding a layer of complexity to the conversation. Hugh remained silent, grappling with the echoes of his past—Ethan's past. William, perceptive as ever, continued to tread carefully through the delicate emotions.

"You never really let go of that, did you? The need for justice?"

Hugh's jaw clenched, and he nodded slowly. "I couldn't. I can't."

The mountain seemed to echo with the weight of the unsolved mystery that had shaped Hugh's life. The events leading to Hugh's transformation into Ethan's alter ego remained vivid, a series of traumatic memories etched into his psyche.

"Ethan gave up on finding who murdered his parents. He wanted to forget, move on. But I won't let him do that. It isn't just about them; it is about every victim who never got justice," Hugh spoke as he looked at Yahia's body, his voice carrying the burden of years spent in pursuit of answers.

A bitter smile played on Hugh's lips. "Sold Ethan's restaurant, started my own agency. I will never let Ethan live a normal life, not after what had happened. I need to do something, make a difference."

The temperature felt colder as memories resurfaced, filling his mind with images of the night Ethan discovered his parents' lifeless bodies, the frustration of an unsolved crime, and the relentless pursuit of justice that consumed Hugh.

William studied Hugh's face, recognizing the deep-seated pain etched in his features. "You think you'll ever find closure?"

"I don't know, but I can't live without trying. It's what makes me exist," Hugh confessed, his eyes holding a glint of anguish.

The sound of wind howling echoed through their ears. The conversation lingered in the air, heavy with the unresolved past that clung to Hugh's every word.

William contemplated the weight of Hugh's burden, Ethan's burden. He could not help but marvel at the complexity of the human mind. Here, on the quiet mountain, two personalities coexisted, each carrying its own tale of pain and resilience.

"Sometimes, change is the only constant. And sometimes, you have to become someone else to discover who you truly are," Hugh said.

William nodded in agreement.

"I'm glad I parted ways with my psychiatry position at your father's office after his passing to stand by your side. My dedication extends to both of you," William conveyed with genuine warmth. "The Ethan Abbott Private Investigation Office is now our path. Thanks to your efforts, Ethan is one of London's premier private investigators, and, oh, well, me too."

However, Hugh remained impassive, unaffected by William's compliment. Behind his stoic exterior, he harboured a conviction that William held a greater fondness for Ethan. Hugh had little regard for his father's psychiatry office, a business Ethan had relinquished to concentrate on the family restaurant. Hugh's singular focus was on the pursuit of justice.

"Let's make our way back to the inn; the authorities need to be informed, and we have to maintain the integrity of the crime scene," Hugh asserted. "We shouldn't let this man lie in the cold any longer."

Hugh turned towards the inn, his determined strides leading the way. Unfazed, William trailed behind, the distance between them accentuating the silent tension that lingered in the air.

## CHAPTER 4: THE ARCHITECTS

Mohammed, the teenage receptionist, who had earlier exhibited a cheerful demeanour that now disappeared, suggested heading to the nearest police station due to the disconnected phone lines. To provide some semblance of dignity, William took charge and covered the deceased with a white sheet. The abruptness of the incident left the tour group in a state of collective disbelief as they waited for law enforcement to arrive, with emotions ranging from shock to grief. Brigitte, tears streaming down her face, found solace in Jacqueline's comforting presence. Soo-Ah, unable to comprehend the grim reality, stood in disbelief. Others within the group sought comfort in each other, their shared sense of bewilderment palpable.

Two local police officers eventually arrived. However, their arrival brought little assurance, as their unprofessionalism and lack of competence cast a shadow over the unfolding investigation. An hour-long delay further heightened the group's anxiety, compelling the local police to instruct everyone to remain at the inn until the nearest city police or capital police could take over. The authorities planned to contact Sinai Bird Travel Agency once the phone lines were restored, prompting Mohammed and Chef Fakhri to temporarily close the inn in the meantime.

"I inspected Yahia's room here at the inn. It appeared untouched; he hadn't even stepped inside. There's nothing noteworthy to find in there," William mentioned.

"I must change out of these clothes immediately," Hugh ignored William, fixing a determined gaze on his reflection in the room's mirror.

In contrast to Ethan, Hugh projected an air of cold detachment and carried himself with a noticeable sense of pride. His words were measured, and his eyes sparkled with intelligence. Neatly styled with a side parting and held in place with gel, Hugh's hair stood as a testament to his meticulous nature. His attire, in stark contrast to Ethan's, unmistakably signalled his profession as a private investigator—a black coat, white shirt, and a black tie, visually proclaiming his detective status.

Exiting the inn, they paused by the entrance's rusty machine to acquire two cups of warm tea.

"Not quite the tea I was hoping for," William remarked, scrutinising the cups.

Hugh, with a teasing smirk, concurred. As they made their way to the outdoor seating area, Derek anxiously sat on the top rail of one of the couches, where Hugh and William joined him. Just as William was about to take a sip, Hugh deftly intercepted the cup, passing it to Derek. William made a slight, frustrated gesture.

"Nice outfit," Derek complimented, eyeing Hugh's detective attire."

"What happened?" Observing Derek's freshly wrapped palm, Hugh inquired about the injury.

"My hand? Oh, I had a mishap breaking a glass in our room," he explained, shaking his left leg uncontrollably.

"It looks like you're still in shock," Hugh gently began, perceiving Derek's unease.

Unable to meet Hugh's gaze, Derek admitted, "I don't typically encounter dead bodies, you know?" his voice laced with sarcasm, revealing a hint of quivering unease.

"I've noticed you and Yahia haven't exchanged many words during the tour," William remarked.

"What are you implying?" Derek retorted in frustration.

"Not insinuating anything, just fulfilling my duty to ensure everyone's safety. Besides, it'll save you time when the police call us all for questioning," William stated.

A few moments of silence went by.

"We had a fallout over my father offering Yahia a job. Two months back, my father and I visited Egypt. He's a highly accomplished architect in Japan, with businesses spanning multiple countries, including here. It was meant to be a routine business trip turned sightseeing tour lasting four days. Yahia was our guide, and let's say, he left a big impression on my father. My father even offered him a job as a translator in his company. I heard Yahia turned down the offer." Finding solace in being finally heard, Derek told his tale to Hugh and William, who listened without offering much response.

"It's rather unfortunate, isn't it? Yahia secures a position in your father's company, while you weren't good enough to make it there. Jealousy. If you ask me, that's good reason to murder someone," Hugh remarked with a cool detachment and sarcasm.

"Hey, I would never commit murder, even if I'm not good enough," Derek declared, locking eyes with Hugh. However, Hugh, renowned for his intense stares, maintained his gaze until Derek eventually looked away.

Hugh took a moment, sipping his now lukewarm tea, while Derek remained still, not even touching his.

"What a waste," William muttered quietly, eyeing the cup of tea in Derek's hand to diffuse the tension. Both Hugh and Derek glanced at William briefly.

"While I'm aware of your roles as private investigators, I am not obligated to respond to any of your questions, especially if they come with unfounded accusations. We should let the Egyptian authorities handle this matter," Derek asserted as he got up to leave.

"Derek, come on," William implored, reaching out his arms to gently restrain Derek from leaving. "I understand. We didn't mean to imply anything. We just want everyone to feel safe. Whether there's a murderer among us or not, it's best for everyone to keep a low profile until the police arrive, right?"

Derek sighed, contemplating the suggestion for a moment, eventually giving in.

"How did you come across the body?" Hugh inquired.

"After dinner, I spent an hour with the guys and then took a stroll outside with my journal to jot down some thoughts. I returned to our room, changed into my workout gear," his voice quivered slightly. Derek took hold of the cup of tea, swallowed the now-cold liquid, and continued, "I usually engage in a ninety-minute run every day."

"Yes, I remember seeing your regular exercise routine back in Cairo," William concurred.

"I wanted a short break, so I headed to the edge of the mountain for some fresh air, and that's where I discovered him lying there. I nudged him and tried calling his name to wake him, but I soon realised he was dead. That's how I ended up with blood on me. I hurried back to the inn to inform someone," he finished, turning to meet Hugh's gaze. Derek's dark eyes were quite striking. "And like you did; everyone woke up to the commotion."

"Did you move the body?" Hugh asked calmly, briefly glancing at Derek's sports shoe now coated with sand.

"Besides giving him a gentle nudge, no, I did not," replied Derek.

"I suppose we should head back in, maybe engage in a conversation with your two friends. Let's see if they saw anything unusual," Hugh suggested.

Lost in his contemplations, Hugh retraced his steps to the Sunrise Inn, navigating the deserted surroundings with thoughtful observation. The setting seemed tailor-made for a crime, an isolated spot that a cunning killer could exploit while the rest slumbered. Downing his water bottle in one decisive go, an unusual silence settled in, a stark departure from the ambiance since their arrival in Saint Catherine. It felt as if Saint Catherine's soul had departed with Yahia.

As the duo approached Derek's room, shared with his colleagues, they knocked softly. Hugh and William entered the architects' space after a warm welcome from Mike. Jake was present, engrossed in a deep conversation with Mike.

"William, Ethan, please come in," Mike greeted warmly.

"Your room is quite snug," Hugh remarked, his gaze roaming the room.

"Is this about Yahia?" Jake regarded Hugh with an uncomfortable curiosity.

William nodded.

"The poor chap had to endure such a brutal fate. Shocking. The notion of sharing space with a murderer is unsettling to say the least." Transitioning to a more solemn demeanour, Mike remarked as he steered clear of direct eye contact with Hugh.

"It could be anyone, can't it? This situation is ludicrous. The phone lines are down, and those who arrived earlier hardly match the criteria for real police. They barely did anything," Jake interjected.

Hugh attentively absorbed their dialogue, surveying the somewhat stifling room and the empty trash. Despite its status as a men's enclave, it maintained a surprising tidiness, a feat considering the recent check-in. Derek's dinner attire was neatly arranged on his bed.

"Poor Derek," Mike sighed, a touch of sympathy in his voice. "He appeared truly shaken upon discovering the body. It must have been an immense shock, especially considering his acquaintance with Yahia."

"It undoubtedly was," William concurred, his concern mirrored in his expression. "What were your activities after dinner?"

"We headed back to the room, engaged in conversation, attempted to watch TV despite the poor signal—mostly national channels that were unintelligible." Mike gestured towards the television. "Derek left about an hour later for his routine evening walk; he's pretty devoted to his writing."

"Did you happen to see anything out of the ordinary during or after dinner?" Hugh probed.

Jake sat up abruptly, his eyes lighting up with a sudden recollection. "Yes!" he exclaimed. With animated gestures, he began to recount the events.

"I woke up a little after midnight, desperately needing to use the bathroom. Derek hadn't returned by then. Mike asked me to adjust the heater in our room. After sorting that out, I made my way to the hallway where the shared bathroom is. Our room isn't an ensuite as you can see. There was this eerie silence that surrounded me, a stillness suggesting that everyone was either asleep, absent from the inn, or unusually quiet in their rooms. I could hear my own heartbeat."

He swallowed and continued, "I saw Yahia and started calling out to him as I got closer. But the moment he heard his name, he ducked away, making me go after him. It was like he was trying to put distance between us. When I finally swung open the door to the study room he ducked into, he was gone. Just the curtains, flapping wildly in the gusting wind from the open window."

With wide eyes and earnest nods, Jake shared his experience, crafting a suspenseful tale for Hugh, William, and Mike.

"Why did he run when you called out to him?" Mike questioned eagerly.

"Maybe he was apprehensive? Maybe he felt the murderer nearby and fear took hold!" Jake concluded in response to his own speculative musings.

## CHAPTER 5: *MULUKHIYAH*, CHICKEN, AND RICE

The next day unfolded, with Mohammed and Chef Fakhri of the Sunrise Inn diligently attending to the tour group, adhering to the updated instructions of the local police to await the travel agency's bus for the journey from the Inn in Saint Catherine back to Cairo. Despite finding comfort in William and Ethan's company and having faith in their private investigator acumen to navigate the situation, the tour group remained oblivious to the fact that it was Hugh providing protection, not Ethan. As the clock struck lunchtime, the tantalizing aroma emanating from the inn's kitchen lured Hugh in that direction.

The modest kitchen at the Sunrise Inn radiated an air of simplicity and warmth. Compact in size, it held an array of mismatched utensils that bore the marks of time and use. The aroma of spices lingered, a testament to the culinary prowess of Chef Fakhri. Recollections of Ethan's family restaurant remained, but Hugh endeavoured to dispel those memories from Ethan's consciousness—his consciousness. The worn wooden cabinets, painted in a soft shade of cream, housed an assortment of herbs and ingredients neatly arranged in glass jars. The kitchen, though unassuming, emanated a sense of comfort and familiarity, its simplicity belying the richness of the culinary creations that emerged from its humble confines.

Hugh found his attention drawn to a vintage clock on the wall. Its hands ticking with a rhythmic precision, overseeing the culinary symphony that unfolded within the confined space. The vintage clock triggered elusive memories just beyond his reach. A distant recollection of a watch lingered in Hugh's memories, refusing to fully manifest itself.

"That smell is tempting. What culinary masterpiece is in the making?" Hugh inquired with a feigned warmth that masked his usual reserved demeanour. Engaging with people wasn't his forte, but he knew it was a necessary means to an end.

Chef Fakhri, clad in a slightly stained olive-green shirt bearing traces of flour and charcoal, paired with rugged black trousers, defied the conventional image of a chef's pristine attire. Hugh couldn't help but mull over the fortune that spared restaurant patrons from witnessing the less glamorous side of kitchen staff. The old chef face had intricate wrinkles that resembled detailed maps, each telling the story of his rich life experiences. Despite the years etched on his features, a surprisingly youthful spirit seemed to reside beneath.

"The best I can make. Egyptian *mulukhiyah* and roasted chicken," he declared, engrossed in the culinary process.

Hugh attentively watched Chef Fakhri expertly handle the *mulukhiyah* leaves. "These leaves transform into a thick, somewhat soupy mixture when cooked. That's what *mulukhiyah* is," explained the seasoned chef, shedding light on the essence of the dish.

"Well, old man, your culinary skills could easily draw in a considerable clientele," Hugh remarked, acknowledging Chef Fakhri's culinary prowess, reciprocated by a warm smile from the seasoned chef.

"Did you manage to get a good night's sleep?" Hugh gently inquired, his probing tone attempting to unravel the events of the previous night.

"I doubt anyone did," Chef Fakhri responded, displaying perceptiveness that swiftly identified Hugh's investigative nature. As they delved into a conversation about Yahia's transformation over the past six months, the chef's countenance turned sombre, lost in contemplation.

"And where were you when Yahia met his unfortunate fate last night?" Hugh pressed, his questioning gaze fixed on Chef Fakhri.

"I was tidying up the seating area after dinner, also tending to the charcoal. I headed inside the inn to retire to my room for some rest. As usual, Mohammed was dozing off at the front desk due to his long working hours," the chef explained, offering a glimpse into his routine on that fateful night.

"So, how does it work? Do you and Mohammed take shifts? I've noticed only the two of you here," Hugh asked.

"Yes, we take shifts. Life's hardships force responsibility on people like me and Mohammed," Chef Fakhri explained. "I have three sons, all thriving in the police force in Cairo, and one of them is getting married soon. My daughters, however, are still trapped with me here. After my wife passed away, I found myself in a difficult financial situation. All I want is to provide a better life for my daughters and make my sons proud."

Mohammed interrupted their conversation as he entered with a heavy sack of charcoal. Chef Fakhri directed him to fetch soft drinks, signalling that lunch was almost ready.

"I'll join you, if that's alright?" Hugh stated to Mohammed, with a clear disregard for the possibility of Mohammed having a different opinion. "I need to refill my water bottle. Tap water doesn't suit my taste." His intent was evident; he would go regardless of the reception.

Mohammed, respectful and courteous, walked alongside Hugh, demonstrating deference to his elders.

Hugh managed to force a smile. "How long have you been working here?"

"It's been a year. I come from Yahia's hometown," replied the dark-skinned receptionist. "It's a small town down south."

The storage room, a compact space, unfolded before Hugh's eyes as Mohammed swung the door open. Shelves, neatly arranged, held an assortment of soft drinks and juices, their vibrant labels forming a colourful mosaic. The room emanated an organized simplicity, each item having its designated place, creating a harmonious coexistence within the confined quarters.

"Do you know Yahia well?"

"My older brother was a mate of his. Sadly, he passed away in a bus accident two years ago," Mohammed revealed, his voice carrying a note of solemnity as Hugh sipped on his water.

"Yahia held a solid reputation in our town and at work. I don't understand who would commit such a heinous act against such a good person. Unlike..." Mohammed hesitated.

"Unlike what?" Hugh probed.

"Unlike deceitful individuals who live double lives. He did nothing wrong," Mohammed staunchly defended, "and now, Sir, we should go. I don't want to get scolded by Chef Fakhri."

Hugh acquiesced to the teenager. Despite his considerable ego, he disliked relinquishing control of a situation. Hugh navigated to the lunchroom where many in the group had congregated as lunch was being served by Chef Fakhri and Mohammed. Observing William already seated, he chose a chair nearby. William stared at him sceptically, and Hugh met his gaze nonchalantly.

"Where were you?" William whispered.

"Conducting my interrogations while someone lounged in the dining area with the ladies," Hugh replied, crossing his legs and casually tossing the plastic bottle onto the table.

He smirked, relishing the opportunity to tease William. "Oh, please." William rolled his eyes, though Hugh's teasing could occasionally grate on his nerves.

"So, where's that French girl who's also a tour guide?"

"Since you weren't around, let me update you," William said calmly. He had the highest tolerance for Hugh, but there were times when he pushed every last nerve William had. "She's locked herself in her room. Jacqueline mentioned she's not eating. That probably explains it."

"More food for us then," Hugh remarked without a hint of compassion.

Later, everyone gathered around the dining table, except Brigitte, who chose to skip the meal, and Mrs Flavia Hottinger and Mr Nico Hottinger, who were still getting ready in their room. Hugh quietly began indulging in the succulent roasted chicken thigh. Daniela, he observed, hardly touched her food.

"Isn't Brigitte having lunch? She hasn't eaten since yesterday," Jake inquired of Jacqueline between mouthfuls, ever the eager conversationalist.

"I tried to convince her, but she's holding out for the police to arrive so we can all return to Cairo," Jacqueline replied, her gaze descending to her plate.

"She's missing out," Hugh remarked icily, sipping his soup. A nudge from William prompted Hugh to cast a disgusted look in his direction.

"You're quite the mystery, Detective Ethan," Derek remarked casually. "You've been unusually sarcastic and reserved since the murder. Your voice is even deeper. What a change from the loud, outspoken person we've known for weeks."

Hugh emphatically placed his spoon on the table, sitting up with a dignified posture, engaging in an intense gaze with Derek. It marked their second formidable stare-down until, once again, Derek relented, feeling the discomfort under Hugh's scrutiny. Hugh nonchalantly wiped soup from his lips with his thumb, maintaining his fixed gaze on Derek, who shifted awkwardly under the penetrating examination.

Thanks to Mrs Hottinger's arrival, Derek finally got a break from Hugh's intense gaze as his attention shifted towards her. She entered the lunchroom last, rushing in with Mr Hottinger, and her furious demeanour caused a bit of chaos in the room.

"My diamond ring! It's gone! Our family heirloom!" she yelled in panic.

"Good gracious, that's piercing," Hugh murmured to William, his temples pulsating. The headache was escalating with each passing moment. "Not again, this infernal headache..."

William firmly grasped Hugh's arms, attempting to guide him back. But it wasn't Ethan... his eyes were different... older... wiser...

Time seemed to stand still, with only William and Hugh existing within its confines. The others appeared as blurry spectacles in the background, drawn to Mrs Hottinger's tumultuous arrival.

"Ethan?" William whispered.

"It's Charles, son..."

"Charles...? Why...? Why are you here...?"

"Something lured me in, a memory," Charles explained, but suddenly, the headache struck again.

"What's going on? No, wait… please don't go just yet…" William pleaded.

In a matter of seconds, Ethan opened his eyes. The familiar gaze of his friend had replaced Charles'. The person William had desperately wished to linger was no more, leaving behind an enigmatic void.

## CHAPTER 6: FOOTBALL GAME

The commotion was about the lost ring—Mrs Hottinger's grandmother's heirloom passed down through generations. Mr Hottinger had discovered it was missing while him and his sister were getting ready. The ring caught the attention of all the women in the tour group. Ethan and William remembered last week, during a coffee break in a quaint Cairo café, how Brigitte admired Mrs Hottinger's ring. "Wow, Mrs Hottinger, this ring is stunning. The ruby shines, and those pearls around it... simply lovely," she exclaimed. The other ladies echoed similar sentiments. "It must cost a fortune," Soo Ah had added. Mrs Hottinger basked in the compliments, precisely what she wanted. However, the ring is now missing.

"Where is it?!" Mr Hottinger's voice echoed through the room, cutting through the ambient noise. The other tourists looked up, their curious eyes turning towards the furious man. The tension in the air was palpable.

Mrs Hottinger clasped her hands together, tears welling up in her eyes. "I must've dropped it somewhere."

"Let's find it!" Jacqueline, always quick on her feet, declared, standing up from her chair. The others followed suit, eager to help.

Jake suggested, "Maybe it slipped off during dinner. Check under the tables."

The tourists dispersed, each taking a designated area to search. Mrs Hottinger remained near her brother, her hands trembling. Soo Ah and Jun Hyuk inspected the chairs, lifting cushions and peering underneath. Mike, with his towering stature, scanned the room for any glint of the missing ring. William and Ethan also joined.

The search unfolded quietly, interrupted only by whispered conversations among the tourists. The inn, once vibrant with conversation, now echoed with the cautious footsteps of those looking for the lost heirloom.

Despite their collective efforts, the ring remained elusive. The atmosphere grew heavier with each passing moment, disappointment etched on the faces of the tourists. Mrs Hottinger, still visibly upset, exchanged glances with her brother.

Ethan, after an hour of searching with the group, decided to break the tension. "How about we take a break from searching? Maybe a change of scene will help lighten the mood."

The suggestion was met with puzzled looks, but Ethan continued, "I've noticed there's an empty field outdoors. How about we gather there for a friendly football game? It might be a good way to distract ourselves and lift our spirits."

Jacqueline, always one for positive energy, perked up. "That sounds like a great idea! A bit of fresh air and physical activity might be just what we need."

"How about the Hottingers?" Ethan directed his eyes towards the siblings.

Amidst the encouragement and agreement from others, Mr Hottinger found himself caught up in the light-hearted atmosphere. His initial anger had melted away, replaced by a sense of solidarity with the other tourists.

Daniela, sensitive to her aunt's emotions, approached her with a comforting smile. "Don't worry too much, Aunt Flavia. These things happen, and I'm sure the ring will turn up eventually."

Mrs Hottinger forced a weak smile, appreciating Daniela's attempt to console her. "I just can't believe I lost it. It's been in the family for generations."

Mr Hottinger placed a gentle hand on his sister's shoulder. "Flavia, I'm sorry for getting angry. It was just the initial panic. We'll find a way to replace the ring, or perhaps it's a sign that it was meant to be lost."

Ethan smiled at the reconciliation of the brother and sister. He then headed to Jake, who had just finished a can of Coke. He crushed the can and said, "This can be our ball. We've seen it in Cairo, kids playing their own game, with their own ball. Who needs one when you've got this?" He winked at Daniela, but she didn't smile.

"You're expecting *all* of us to play football?" Jun Hyuk jested, his laughter fading into the realisation of a muted response from the others.

"Why not *all* of us?" Soo Ah retorted, her gaze lingering on her husband, a playful challenge in her eyes.

"I'll sit this one out. I've had too much to eat for lunch," William declared, opting for the side-lines.

The sandy outdoors provided a vast canvas for their impromptu football match. As the afternoon sun cast a warm golden hue over the landscape, the grains of sand seemed to shimmer like scattered gold dust. The distant mountains stood sentinel; their jagged peaks softened by the gentle embrace of sunlight. A cold breeze carried the earthy scent of the desert, enhancing the tranquil atmosphere. Using rocks to mark makeshift goals, Ethan, Mike, Jake, and Jun-Hyuk transformed the sandy canvas into a spirited playground.

The teams were meticulously crafted: Mike, Derek, Jacqueline, and Soo Ah comprised one side, while Ethan,

Daniela, Jun Hyuk, and Jake formed the opposing team. William and the Hottingers chose to assume the roles of intrigued spectators. William observed how Derek gazed at Jacqueline, his eyes reflecting a blend of admiration and profound bashfulness.

"I find the match quite amusing," remarked William, sharing a seat next to Mr and Mrs Hottinger. The Hottingers, with anticipation in their eyes, observed the football spectacle, hopeful that Daniela would forge connections and create lasting memories.

"Mr Hottinger, you have a remarkably talented daughter," William acknowledged, initiating a conversation. To their surprise, Daniela exhibited exceptional prowess on the sandy pitch. Mr Hottinger glowed with pride, his daughter's athleticism surpassing expectations.

"I certainly do," Mr Hottinger replied, maintaining unwavering focus on Daniela's agile movements. Despite her serious demeanour during the game, a radiant smile illuminated her face when she successfully scored a goal. William swore it was the first time he'd seen her smile.

"Her mum passed away four years ago, and Flavia's husband followed a year later. Since then, we've been living together," Mr Hottinger disclosed. "My disability, as you can see, limits my ability to engage in many activities with my daughter." He gestured towards his cane, resting on the plastic chair.

"You know I am always here for you and Daniela," Mrs Hottinger assured, placing one hand on her brother's knee to comfort him, to which he nodded.

"I worry about Daniela. The murder probably hit her hard. She hardly eats, and nothing seems to lift her spirits. We're in Egypt, for heaven's sake, but her mental health seems to be deteriorating," Mr Hottinger expressed, rubbing his knees with a sense of concern.

"Nico, please. Daniela will be okay. I know this is tough on her, but it's affecting all of us," Mrs Hottinger replied.

Mrs Hottinger always had a polished appearance, wearing beige trousers and a white knitted sweater that complemented her black eyes, with her short black hair neatly styled. Her nails were carefully painted with metallic red nail polish, and she prudently adorned herself with pearl earrings from her jewellery box.

"Now, excuse me, gentlemen. I'll head inside to get a shawl; it's too cold." Mrs Hottinger rubbed her arms with her two hands and rose from her seat, making her way towards the inn.

"I did tell her to dress warmly, you know. But it's always style over comfort for Flavia."

William and Mr Hottinger shared a laugh and continued watching the game.

"Her anxiety isn't a major concern. I've treated many with severe anxiety. I'm not just a doctor; I'm a lifesaver," commented William, applauding Derek, who nearly scored. "Perhaps I can look into her case. Even though we're here for a short while, I might be able to help."

Laughter and banter echoed amidst the teams, creating a contrasting ambiance against the serene backdrop of the desert landscape.

"You seem confident. Have you ever failed to help a patient?" Mr Hottinger inquired, momentarily diverting his attention from the unfolding football drama.

"I wouldn't say I have failed, but I haven't succeeded yet. A case—unusual, challenging—made me question my ethics and principles," William replied, his voice carrying a hint of introspection.

"We sure will come find you if we need you," Mr Hottinger acknowledged with a nod, though the offered assistance lingered like a subtle promise.

"Please do," William affirmed.

"Oh, look, Flavia is returning with her shawl," Mr Hottinger chuckled, observing his sister's graceful approach back to the group.

Soo Ah and Jacqueline happily exchanged a high-five, revelling in their win. On the opposing side, Ethan's team faced defeat, leaving Daniela and Jun Hyuk visibly displeased, assigning blame to Ethan and Jake for the lacklustre performance. Ethan adopted a defensive stance, hands on hips, asserting that he never professed to be the team's star player. Daniela and Jun Hyuk exchanged groans, unconvinced by Ethan's explanation. Despite the exertion that left him sweating, Ethan hadn't made significant contributions to the game.

Victory brought a satisfying sense of accomplishment, even in the simplicity of the moment. Ethan mused, observing the jubilant celebration of the winning team while reclining on the sandy ground, weary from exertion. William reached out his arms towards Ethan, who gratefully accepted the offered assistance.

"If Hugh were here, he would've clinched the win, you know," William playfully taunted.

"Oh, spare me," Ethan retorted, hauling himself back up onto his feet. He nodded towards the Hottingers, who were rallying around Daniela after her team's loss.

"What was the conversation all about?" Ethan inquired.

"Let me fill you in as we head back inside. It's getting rather cold."

As they strolled back towards the inn, the sun dipped lower in the sky, forming a warm glow over the desert landscape and Ethan found himself ensnared in the clutches of a pounding headache.

"Are you okay?" William asked as he extended a steadying hand. The warmth of William's touch, a fleeting anchor amidst the storm clearly brewing within Ethan's mind, offered a momentary respite.

"Stop, Hugh... No, stop..." Ethan grappled with himself.

*Don't resist, Ethan... I'm always going to be here...*

A few moments later, Ethan was calm.

"I must change out of these garments, Dr Harrington," Hugh said as he coaxed Ethan back into slumber.

## CHAPTER 7: BREAKING NEWS

In the study room of the Sunrise Inn, Brigitte appeared before the others for the first time since the murder. Her typically vibrant aura, adorned with make-up and vivacity, was evidently absent.

The group gathered around the TV that flickered in the corner, its screen struggling to illuminate the room's sombre atmosphere. The faint glow of the screen cast shadows upon Brigitte's face as she navigated through the channels; her fingers moved with a sense of urgency, as if each button press was an attempt to escape the harsh reality that surrounded them.

After several aggressive adjustments, Brigitte's face, illuminated by the glow of the television, finally broke into an exclamation. "A signal!" Her voice, though triumphant, carried an undertone of exhaustion. The flickering screen, now showing a national news channel, that aired news in Arabic.

"Mohammed!" she called out to the fourteen-year-old, who rushed in.

"What's the news saying?" she asked.

Mohammed wore a concerned expression as he conveyed the news anchor's message.

*"In a surprising turn of events, the Cairo Museum has reported the disappearance of a golden Ankh, a priceless artefact with significant historical and cultural value. The delicate and intricately crafted symbol of life and immortality has vanished from its display, leaving both museum officials and the public stunned. The police have been called in to investigate this puzzling incident, treating the disappearance as a matter of great importance due to the historical significance of the stolen relic. The museum, usually a haven for ancient treasures, now finds itself at the centre of a mystery that has left both authorities and curators grappling for answers. As the investigation unfolds, the fate of the missing Ankh hangs in the balance, with the hope that the symbol of life will soon be restored to its rightful place in the heart of Cairo's rich cultural heritage."*

"That's ludicrous!" Mike responded to the news.

"Tell me about it. Reminds me of the Montreal Museum of Fine Arts robbery. They swiped 18 paintings!" Derek exclaimed.

"Yeah, fortunate that they only nabbed a single item from the Egyptian Museum," Mike said.

"Guys, wasn't the object that tumbled from Yahia's bag an Ankh? I think it was… I've watched enough documentaries to identify it," Jake asserted, his eyes narrowing as he addressed the diverse group of tourists.

"It looked pretty similar," Mrs Hottinger agreed.

Mr Hottinger, sitting nearby with his cane, appeared less convinced. "Well, Flavia, it could have been anything. I don't think any of us saw it clearly."

Jacqueline chimed in, her eyes reflecting uncertainty. "Soo-Ah mentioned reading somewhere that owning an Egyptian ornament could assist a woman unable to bear children in conceiving, right, Soo Ah?'

"Ah… yeah yeah…" Soo Ah said nervously. "But…but it didn't look like an Egyptian ornament."

"I second that," William agreed.

Jun Hyuk leaned back in his chair. "Could have been a random trinket. People carry all sorts of things in their bags."

"I agree. It wasn't an Ankh. I've seen many Ankhs in real life and in history books," Brigitte said, clearly irritated. "Why are we fussing over an object? We're not detectives. Leave it to the professionals."

"No harm in discussing it. Right, detectives?" Jake disagreed as he shifted his gaze towards Hugh and William.

Hugh yawned without saying a word.

"I like your enthusiasm," William said to Jake.

"Let's not jump to conclusions. None of us took a good look at it. And even if it was, how is it relevant to what happened?" Mr Hottinger added his two cents.

The discussion continued, each member of the group presenting their perspective. The room buzzed with a blend of curiosity, uncertainty, and a collective desire for resolution that was interrupted when Mohammed's face reddened with panic as he shifted his gaze towards the breaking report that came in through the television.

"Now what?" Brigitte questioned.

"An earthquake struck the capital," Mohammed said. And he found himself translating once again.

*"The 5.8 magnitude earthquake hit Cairo at exactly 15:09. The destructive earthquake caused 545 deaths and almost 6,512 injuries. The damages caused left almost 50,000 people homeless. 212 historic monuments have been affected in Cairo as a result of the unexpected earthquake. The Great Pyramid of Giza has lost a block during the shake. The aftershock has protracted..."*

"I must go to the nearby police station for updates on Cairo's situation," Mohammed declared, swiftly departing from the seating area.

The group anxiously awaited Mohammed's return, and upon his comeback, he brought news that the Cairo police might arrive the following day, possibly by evening, due to the situation in the capital. The announcement of the delayed police arrival triggered an immediate physical response from Brigitte. Her usually poised composure shattered, revealing a display of visceral frustration. A subtle quiver in her lips and the clenching of her jaw betrayed the turmoil within. Tension emanated from her every movement as she clenched and unclenched her fists, fingers tightly interlocking in an expression of defiance.

The seating area, now charged with the electric energy of anger and complaints, seemed to close in around the group as they grappled with mounting impatience and helplessness. Mike, on the other hand, optimistically noted their luck in not being in the capital during the earthquake, aiming to uplift everyone's spirits. Eventually, the group dismantled from the seating area, leaving only a trio behind: Hugh, William, and the self-proclaimed investigator. Jake remained seated. The flickering TV cast shadows on their faces as they huddled over a small table.

Jake, with piercing blue eyes and tousled blonde hair, presented himself to the group with a casual yet eclectic style. He donned a fitted denim jacket over a well-worn graphic tee, embracing an effortless blend of rugged charm and youthful energy. Despite the tense atmosphere, Jake exuded a certain laid-back confidence. His easy-going demeanour, coupled with an irrepressible enthusiasm for mystery and crime.

Jake eagerly offered his insights. "I've been thinking, detectives. This murder mystery we've got here, it's like something out of those documentaries I watch. I can help."

Hugh, with his characteristic scepticism, raised an eyebrow. "We're not characters in one of your documentaries. This is real life."

William, the voice of reason, added, "And in the real world, matters are seldom as straightforward as they appear in your beloved documentaries."

"But they always say, follow the motive," Jake persisted. "I can't see any of us having a motive to kill Yahia. He was well-liked."

Hugh scoffed, "People often harbour concealed motives. Just because you can't recognise them doesn't mean they don't exist."

Jake, undeterred, continued, "And another thing, what could be the murder weapon? No sharp objects around here match the wound on Yahia's head. The murderer must have gotten rid of it."

William sighed, "What makes you certain the murderer isn't among us?'

"No motive! It must be someone from outside the group. We're unaware of Yahia's life beyond work, you know," Jake asserted. "Alternatively, it could be the receptionist or the chef; they already have some history with Yahia."

"Derek had a prior relationship with Yahia, too, you know," Hugh remarked.

"Are you genuinely suspecting him? I know Derek; he would never," Jake responded with an earnest defence of his friend.

Hugh scrutinised Jake with a disapproving gaze, unwelcoming of his suggestions. His ego bristled at the thought of someone meddling in his investigations.

William leaned back, crossing his arms. "At times, motives aren't immediately obvious."

Jake, undeterred, remained resolute in showcasing his investigative prowess. "No, no, no. I've seen enough of these documentaries to understand that there's always an apparent motive. We just need to dig deeper."

"We?" Hugh smirked.

William tried to downplay Hugh's sarcasm in the conversation. "Jake, exercise caution and allow the professionals to handle the investigation."

But Jake wasn't one to back down easily. "I'm just saying, we should rule out the possibility that the murderer is among the tourists."

With a smirk, Hugh retorted, "Amateur sleuthing won't be of any help, I assure you."

"Nevertheless," William interjected, "if you happen to notice anything unusual or come across a clue, do let us know. We appreciate your involvement."

## CHAPTER 8: THE TRADITIONAL MARKET

In the evening, after everyone had rested for a while, Mrs Hottinger sat enjoying her tea while engrossed in a romance novel. Her nicely styled hair complemented the navy-blue dress she wore, and a beige jacket was placed elegantly over her shoulders. Hugh quietly took a seat beside her, surprised by her sudden calmness following a noon filled with tears. In about fifteen minutes, William joined them; it seemed imperative for him to be present without any room for error.

"Oh, William! I see you're always by Ethan's side," Mrs Hottinger remarked, gesturing towards Hugh. William didn't appear flattered by the comment. It was only natural for two people travelling together to stick together. Despite the heroism in what he was doing, no one quite understood why William remained attached to Ethan like glue. Hugh on the other hand, couldn't help but grin at the slight jab aimed at William.

Glancing at Mrs Hottinger's book, Hugh read, "*Moonlight Conviction*."

"Ah, yes, a wonderful book. This is my second time reading it," she chuckled. "I know it's not really the time for laughter, but I could use a good laugh after all the unfortunate incidents," she added, setting the book down on the nearby coffee table and picking up her navy-blue teacup.

Hugh couldn't help but notice the array of jewellery she wore, from a pearl necklace to a gold snake bracelet and everything in between.

"I hope I find my grandmother's ring. It's a family heirloom, meant for my dear Daniela. You know, I'm not married nor have any children, but Daniela is like a daughter to me," she said, her eyes getting a little teary. "After the murder of the tour guide, I haven't been able to shut my eyes, not even once. I want to leave this place immediately, and now this earthquake. Hopefully, the police will arrive tomorrow. Nothing seems to go right for me. I married one of Switzerland's wealthiest businessmen at twenty-five. His demanding work led to the narrative of us not having children, and his death in an accident ten years later shocked me. But you know what shocked me even more? His will. He left everything to his mistress, a woman I had no knowledge of until after his death. His betrayal left me devastated, and I lived with my brother and niece ever since."

"I am so sorry to hear you went through this," William said in solidarity.

Hugh remained silent for a few seconds before asking, "Mrs Hottinger, are there any reasons for you to believe that someone might have stolen your diamond ring?"

She put her teacup back on the table, avoiding eye contact. "Well... anyone could have taken it, Ethan. It's a diamond ring, after all."

She glanced around, ensuring no one else overheard, then looked at William.

"William, you seem trustworthy. Can I trust him, too?"

"Of course, Mrs Hottinger. You can rely on him completely."

Mrs Hottinger hesitated, remaining silent for a few moments before revealing what seemed to trouble her.

"Actually, I think it might be my own niece," she confessed.

William and Hugh looked perplexed.

She stumbled over her words at first but eventually explained, "My beloved Daniela is receiving treatment for substance use. Her recovery is going well, but what if she decided to relapse and use my ring to purchase these harmful drugs?" She paused and then continued, "I somewhat regret making a fuss about it. I plan to talk to Daniela about this—"

Her sentence was cut short by Jun Hyuk and Soo Ah entering the room, followed by Mohammed who was with them as a guide. They carried numerous bags, conversing in Korean with surprised expressions. Jun Hyuk set the bags down and turned to the trio in the living room.

"Soo Ah claims she spotted Yahia at the market, about six kilometres away from here," Jun Hyuk stated, while Soo Ah nodded in agreement.

"I'm certain it was him! He was looking around, and our eyes met," Soo Ah added, sounding anxious.

Mrs Hottinger looked directly at the couple, "It can't be him. That's not possible. We clearly saw the body, and the police took it away."

"Perhaps it's his spirit seeking justice for the murder…" Soo Ah nervously responded.

Mohammed remained silent.

"Did you see him, too?" Hugh inquired, addressing Mohammed.

"Um… no," Mohammed replied, avoiding eye contact.

"Take us to the market. It's time we buy some souvenirs for friends back home. What do you think, Dr Harrington?" Hugh suggested, his gaze fixed solely on Mohammed.

The market was bustling. The air was rich with the aroma of exotic spices and the lively chatter of traders bargaining in Arabic. It was adorned with colourful fabrics swaying in the breeze, showcasing complex blue and yellow patterns and textures that spoke of Egypt's ancient weaving traditions. Ornate gold and silver jewellery sparkled, captivating William with their intricate designs and history-laden significance. Handcrafted leather bags, embroidered with intricate Egyptian motifs, hung elegantly alongside the stalls. The atmosphere was a tapestry of sights and sounds.

Hugh couldn't help but notice the air of disappointment surrounding William, as if he wished for nothing more than an undisturbed vacation. It irked Hugh, this silent longing for what could have been, because, despite himself, he found a sense of satisfaction in the disruption.

Mohammed lingered at a nearby café while they headed towards the shop the Korean couple had previously explored. Jun Hyuk had mentioned it was the sole establishment offering tea sets and cups in the surrounding area. A spirited young man vigorously promoted his wares to entice tourists, his voice resounding in a multitude of languages. He enthusiastically beckoned visitors with phrases in diverse tongues, inviting them to inspect his collection. Hugh found this multilingual display quite remarkable.

As Hugh and William approached, the young man energetically called out, "English? Welcome, welcome!"

Hugh shot him a disapproving glance and inquired in a chilly tone, "Have you seen a local man, mid-30s, 175 centimetres in height, brown eyes and hair, in a white shirt, black jersey, with a number nine on it?" Hugh detailed Yahia's appearance as Jun-Hyuk and Soo Ah had described.

The young man raised his eyebrows.

"I see countless people daily; expecting me to recall one who likely didn't buy anything? I remember those who purchase souvenirs, and I can assure you none of them are locals," he retorted sarcastically, urging Hugh and William to leave. "You're disrupting my business."

"Come on, let's go," William urged as the two men exited the shop.

Hugh maintained his disdainful expression until he averted his gaze entirely from the exterior of the shop to the sandy ground. A familiar handkerchief with three exquisitely knitted butterflies in each corner lay beneath his shoe.

"This handkerchief..." William remarked as Hugh picked it up.

"Yes, this handkerchief?" Hugh echoed William's observation.

"The object that fell from Yahia's bag? It was wrapped with this."

"Are you certain?"

"As clear as my knowledge that you are standing before me at this very moment."

Hugh and William arrived at the café where Mohammed awaited them. The unassuming spot boasted a handful of outdoor tables paired with plastic chairs. It appeared to be a vibrant spot in the market, far busier than any other place Hugh had encountered in Saint Catherine city. Shortly after Mohammed prepared to rise from his seat to escort them back to the inn, Hugh gestured for him to stay put, and Mohammed complied.

"Let's share a drink, my treat," Hugh offered, settling onto one of the plastic chairs beside Mohammed.

"What's the best drink for this chilly weather?" Hugh inquired, surveying the modest café surroundings.

"Hmm... *Sahlab*, perhaps?" Mohammed suggested.

"Sah... what? Never mind, let's give it a try," Hugh responded, with William nodding in agreement.

Mohammed then requested three servings of the traditional hot drink. A short while later, a humble waiter served the cups to their table. Hugh admired the distinctly Arabic atmosphere, and William savoured the last sip of this popular Egyptian drink, renowned for its creamy and comforting texture.

"There's something you're not telling us. Don't you think it's time you did?" Hugh said as he crossed his legs.

"Something like what, Sir?"

"Yahia's past, Mohammed," Hugh began, his tone a mix of authority and curiosity. "I need to know more. You seem to be avoiding the topic."

Mohammed, with a faint frown, continued sipping on his *sahlab*, seemingly unresponsive. The breeze ruffled his hair, giving an air of nonchalance, but there was a guarded look in his eyes.

"Yahia was your friend, and his past may hold crucial clues," Hugh pressed, leaning against the table.

Mohammed sighed, his gaze fixed on the distant horizon. "Some things are best left in the past, Sir. Yahia had his reasons for not divulging everything."

Hugh, undeterred, decided to take a different approach. "We need to understand him better to find his murderer. Was there anything unusual about his behaviour recently? Any secrets he confided in you?"

Mohammed paused, glancing at Hugh. "Yahia was a private man. He didn't share much, but lately, he seemed... troubled."

"Troubled how?" Hugh inquired, his gaze steady.

"I don't know…"

"Mohammed, you've known Yahia for quite some time. Don't you want to find his murderer?" William chimed in warmly.

"I'm not sure if I'm supposed to say this. I promised," Mohammed said, casting his gaze downwards.

"It can help," William said.

He remained silent for a few moments. "Yahia had a twin brother," he finally divulged, summoning all his courage to utter the words.

"A twin brother?" William exclaimed in surprise, while Hugh stayed quiet. "He said he didn't have any siblings when Daniela asked him last week during our Nile cruise dinner."

"He has his reasons. When I first met Yahia six months ago during his inaugural tour guiding trip, he made me promise not to mention his twin brother," Mohammed recounted with a tinge of sadness.

"Do you have any inkling as to why he'd make such an unusual request?" William inquired.

"He wanted to sever ties with his past." Hugh stared at Mohammed. "Why would he want to do that? And where is his twin brother now?"

"It's okay, you can answer," William reassured.

"Sir, I don't know... all I know is that after their parents' divorce, their mother passed away from cancer when they were fifteen. They were very different. Yahia was the most helpful person in our town. But Yassine, his twin, led a notorious life filled with drugs and criminality. No one really liked Yassine, but everyone loved Yahia! Naturally, the unwanted attention drawn by Yassine's actions made Yassine leave our hometown, seeking a fresh start in Cairo. Last thing I heard was that Yassine went missing and is presumably dead. Having a brother like him can tarnish your career for good so the least I can do for Yahia is to keep my promise."

The three of them sat there quietly for a minute.

Hugh broke the silence, glanced around, and rose to his feet. "I think it's time we head back. Listen, do not mention anything about the twin brother to the others."

Hugh and William headed back to the inn, finding it was dinner time. Brigitte emerged from her room, engaged in conversation with Jacqueline over *taamiyya* sandwiches they had bought for everyone earlier from the market. Hugh recalled William's mention of how him and Ethan loved those very sandwiches in the streets of Cairo. Hugh could feel it in Ethan's memories, and wanted to try *taamiyya*, too.

He requested to join the ladies for a sandwich. Jacqueline ate her food hastily, as if famished for eons, while Brigitte, in contrast, dined at a slower pace, prompting everyone to wait for her to finish. Hugh savoured his sandwich, grateful Ethan wasn't the one having it; a hint of jealousy lingered as Hugh felt Ethan had better luck with delicious meals, akin to a rivalry, a rivalry that William was treating.

"I see you ladies visited the market earlier today," Hugh remarked, engaging Jacqueline and Brigitte in conversation.

"Absolutely beautiful. Soo Ah and Jun-Hyuk were there, too, but we didn't bump into them," Jacqueline replied with a mouthful, reaching for pickles.

"The murder must be particularly distressing for you," Hugh addressed Brigitte, but her response was silence accompanied by a glare, interpreting Hugh's words as sarcastic. Brigitte's eating resembled a slow-moving turtle, her mind seemingly elsewhere.

"Well, she's making a bit of progress. She was responsive to a man who flirted with her on her way back from the bathroom while I was shopping. Didn't you?" Jacqueline nudged her friend's arm with her elbow as she joked.

"Come on, Jaq," Brigitte smiled momentarily, then the two friends reverted to their sombre expressions.

"It's saddening for all of us, not just Brigitte, right, Brig?" Jacqueline said, prompting Brigitte to nod, almost coerced by Jacqueline's gesture.

"That day, before midnight, we heard cries and screams," Jacqueline recounted, capturing Hugh and William's attention. "Let me start from the beginning. After dinner, Brig retired to our room and I checked out the books in the study area for a while." Brigitte nodded in agreement, indicating her inability to speak, leaving the narrative to Jacqueline.

"I went back to the room later and Brig and I ventured out for hot chocolate with marshmallows. We love our hot chocolate, especially the ones from France, and we had brought our own package from Paris to Egypt. It's a nightly ritual before bed." Jacqueline pushed her hair behind her ears and continued.

"We sat outside in the Bedouin style area, wrapped in blankets, munching on Egyptian seeds we had purchased. Suddenly, we heard loud screams. It was too loud and I dropped my hot chocolate on the ground! Brigitte sprung up and I followed. I was gripping her hand so tightly as we moved towards the commotion." She bit her lip and continued.

"Peering from behind a rock, we saw Jun-Hyuk and Soo Ah. Jun-Hyuk seemed to be calming Soo Ah down. She seemed in distress."

"Do you have any clue why?" William asked.

"No, they were speaking in Korean. But Jun Hyuk seemed pretty anxious and kept urging Soo Ah to hush. He was glancing around apprehensively," Jacqueline replied.

"When they started walking back to the inn, we retreated. We didn't want to intervene, but something didn't feel right," Brigitte finally remarked.

"And then we returned to the room. Brig fell asleep and I couldn't. You know the rest. We met when Derek discovered the body," Jacqueline said.

Hugh felt the return of his headache, gripping his head tightly as Ethan was making a comeback.

## **CHAPTER 9: HUGH WANTS TO KNOW MORE**

After dinner in their shared room, Ethan sat quietly alongside William. William narrated the earlier encounter with Hugh, detailing what had occurred. Ethan listened intently, silently pondering.

"Does he see himself as more intelligent than me?"

William attempted to soothe him, emphasising that if Ethan and the alternate persona continued their struggle for dominance, Ethan's recovery would remain elusive and could spawn other undiscovered personas.

"It's tough for me too, you know. Hugh isn't particularly fond of my company," William quipped.

Understanding the immense challenge of living with an alter ego, William perceived it as a battle for survival. He acknowledged Ethan's limitations in solving crimes independently, recognising that noticing intricate details wasn't his forte, unlike Hugh. Yet, William firmly held on to the belief that despite their differences, Hugh and Ethan were fundamentally the same individual.

"You wish to distance yourself from your parents' murder, but Hugh can't let go," William remarked, choosing his words carefully.

"Is that why he has such disdain for me?" Ethan inquired, seeking clarity.

"He can reciprocate that sentiment about you," William conceded.

"I want to move on; life is much more pleasant without the burden of this constant worry. I want to heal, erase Hugh from existence," Ethan expressed his desire for a fresh start.

"Hugh is a part of who you are, Ethan," William gently reminded.

"He's not. I won't let my illness dictate my existence. The only part of me that matters is Ethan," Ethan declared firmly.

"Attempting to accept Hugh might be the key to finding peace," William suggested.

"I'll never accept him, William. Never," Ethan declared, his resistance unwavering.

It all began when the tragic incident triggered the emergence of Hugh Bennett. It happened within the walls of the Bennett family's residence in Royal Gardens, Kensington Heights, London. Ethan, a mere 21 years old, was jolted awake in the dead of night by a thirst that only a sip of water could quench. Descending to the living room, adjacent to the kitchen, he stumbled upon a gruesome sight: his parents sprawled lifelessly, viciously murdered in a pool of blood. The assailant, draped in black attire and concealed by a mask, made recognition impossible for Ethan.

*Black boots. Black boots bearing a silver star.*

Filled with fear and rage, Ethan dashed out to seek help, but fate had other plans. He tripped over an unopened newspaper at the doorstep, landing with both hands sprawled atop the paper. The headline that met his eyes: *"Actor Hugh Bennett Survives Car Crash in Miraculous Escape."* A sudden, searing headache overcame him, his gaze darkening. Collecting himself, he brushed off the dust from his clothes and strode purposefully to the nearest payphone. Dialling 999, he spoke resolutely, "Hello, this is Detective Hugh Bennett. I'd like to report a murder."

Ethan, now Hugh, glimpsed his reflection in the phone booth. Dissatisfied with how he appeared, he marched to The Gentleman Boutique and strode inside with determination.

Mr Bates, the shop owner acquainted with Ethan's family, was startled by his entrance. Hugh, uncharacteristically silent, fixedly stared without acknowledging Mr Bates.

"Ethan, my lad, I was just closing up. What brings you here?"

Hugh remained quiet, snatching a white shirt and black trousers. He grabbed a black coat from a mannequin and added a black tie to his haul. Mr Bates was taken aback; he had never seen Ethan so imposing, standing squarely before him.

"I'm taking these," Hugh declared. He pierced Mr Bates with a sharp stare.

"That's 500 pounds, Son," stated Mr Bates.

Feeling around Ethan's pockets, he could not find a wallet. However, his hand discovered a round pocket watch. Without hesitation, Hugh handed it to Mr Bates, grabbed the clothes, and departed.

"Son, this is worth so much more!" Mr Bates' fading voice had trailed behind,

In their room, the two friends shared memories, reflecting on how much had changed over time.

"When I discovered that Hugh had handed over my grandfather's pocket watch to Mr Bates, I started visiting The Gentleman Boutique every day, hoping to retrieve it. But shortly after, Mr Bates unexpectedly vanished," Ethan reminisced.

"The shop was taken over by Mr James Collins, right?" William asked.

"Good old Mr Collins," Ethan nodded. "Good old…"

Ethan's temples pulsed with a mounting intensity, a harbinger of the impending headache that loomed. William offered a supportive hand; he knew what was coming. The relentless ache persisted, tightening its grip on Ethan's consciousness. Amid the struggle, Ethan's resolve weakened, and the battle against the encroaching pain became futile. Slowly, almost reluctantly, Ethan succumbed to the overpowering force that was Hugh. The transformation unfolded, casting a shadow over the once vibrant Ethan as the subdued hues of Hugh emerged in the wake of the mental struggle.

"I am the sole authentic being," Hugh declared, his voice resonating with a newfound authority.

"Welcome back," William acknowledged, a tinge of concern lingering in his eyes.

"Let's press on; there's a crime to unravel," Hugh asserted, determination etched on his features as he prepared to delve into the task at hand.

The duo made their way to the seating area. The clock struck 9:00 p.m. and sleep evaded the group, as was often the case since the murder.

Mr Hottinger sat quietly in the seating area, savouring his cup of tea before bed. His white shirt was snugly fitted around his ample belly. Despite not being excessively old, he looked way older than he really was as he always kept his cane close by. The wooden cane's smooth surface, polished to a rich lustre, accentuated the fine grain of the wood. The curvature of the red ebony handle, a testament to ergonomic design, provided not only a supportive grip but also an aesthetic allure.

Seated beside Mr Hottinger on the sofa, Hugh initiated the conversation. "Is there a time where you'll ever stop using the cane?"

"I know, right," chuckled Mr Hottinger before explaining. "It's my right knee; the pain insists I use it along with prescribed medications."

Hugh, intentionally tactless, mentioned, "We've heard about Daniela's struggles from Mrs Hottinger."

Mr Hottinger's expression shifted in surprise and distress. "What?! How could she—"

"Mr Hottinger, please, don't worry. We can keep this between us. We understand," William interjected, seeking to calm him.

Mr Hottinger, easily swayed by William's supportive words, softened. He grew fond of William and felt some comfort in confiding in him.

Mr Hottinger narrated how he was the one who suggested a trip to Egypt, believing it could serve as a restorative getaway for his daughter. Travel held a special place in his heart, and he hoped it might aid in her battle against drug addiction. Sitting with Hugh and William, Mr Hottinger delved into the origins of Daniela's struggle, which began a year prior. Describing Daniela as a courteous and sociable soul, he recalled her birthday celebration—a grand affair arranged by her aunt in his absence due to a business trip.

At the party, one of Daniela's friends introduced drugs to her. Following that incident, Daniela found herself grappling with the clutches of addiction. Over time, she distanced herself from her social circle, seeking solace in prescribed medications to navigate the tumultuous waters of her growing dependence.

"The medications provide some relief, but it's only temporary," Mr Hottinger lamented, taking a sip of his tea.

"Where were you when the murder happened?" Hugh shifted the conversation, inquiring about Mr Hottinger's whereabouts during Yahia's murder.

"I remember retiring to bed while Flavia and Daniela were still out lingering around the inn. I was abruptly awoken by Flavia's complaints about my choice of bed location by the window, forcing us to continue our argument outside to avoid disturbing Daniela."

Mr Hottinger continued, clutching his cane tightly. The audible cracking making Hugh wince.

"I held Yahia in high regard. He was a person of great intellect and pure heartedness. You know? Yahia discussed with me his concern about Daniela's withdrawn nature. He advised me to encourage Daniela to engage in social activities with the tour group and said it would make a difference. What a man… He reassured me and said how fortunate Daniela is to have a father and aunt who love her unconditionally. His kind words will always stay with me," Mr Hottinger said.

Hugh sat, gathering his thoughts while Mike, Derek, and Jake barged in, their boisterous entrance filling the room. Among them, Derek, typically quieter, held a bag of packed pudding.

"Guess what we've got?" Mike exclaimed enthusiastically. "*Omm Ali*, again!" he shouted, unpacking the assortment of smaller packages. Mike handed each person a package. Curiosity piqued, Hugh couldn't resist digging in and Derek slowly savoured the pudding, while Jake expressed how delicious it was, slurping away.

"There's a sombre tale behind this traditional Egyptian dessert," Derek spoke slowly, catching everyone's attention.

"Is it the story you mentioned in the market earlier?" Jake queried, helping himself to more pudding. Derek nodded in confirmation. Hugh noticed a fresh cloth wrapped around Derek's injured wrist, indicating it hadn't fully healed yet.

"*Omm Ali* literally translates to 'the mother of Ali,'" Mr Hottinger chuckled. "I picked up a few Arabic words on this trip," he added.

"Exactly," agreed Mike.

"So, what's the dark story behind it, Derek?" Hugh asked, playfully licking his spoon and keeping eye contact with Derek.

"It involves the first wife of an Egyptian ruler named *Ezz El Din Aybek*, known as the mother of Ali," Derek explained. "She had a rival, Aybek's second wife, named Shagaret El Dorr."

"It's hard enough handling one lady, let alone two," Jake joked, playfully nudging Derek's shoulder.

"Anyway, Shagaret El Dorr orchestrated Aybek's murder and she was later banished and imprisoned. Omm Ali couldn't forgive Shagret El Dorr and got her maids to beat her to death with wooden slippers. To celebrate her death, she asked all the cooks to create the best dessert recipe to distribute all over Egypt and this dish emerged as the winner and was named Omm Ali," Derek continued.

"Except they added a golden coin on each plate as they served the dessert," Mike added, placing his empty bowl on the table.

"No golden coins in here," Mr Hottinger joked; Mike laughed in agreement.

"What a dark story," William said.

"Alright, I need a smoke after this," Mike declared as he finished his pudding.

"Smoking isn't great for you. Any plans to quit?" William muttered, continuing to eat his *Omm Ali* without a hint of remorse for the betrayed deceased woman.

The air was heavy with the scent of aged wood and a faint hint of tobacco lingering from Mike's clothes.

"At times, I reckon I need to pull myself together and quit," Mike admitted. "I've lost count of the number of times I've attempted to kick this nasty habit."

"What's been getting in the way this time?" Hugh asked.

"Stress, mostly. The pressure at work mixed with personal stuff. Smoking has been my crutch for so long; it's like I've forgotten how to stand on my own."

Mike chuckled wryly. "I've tried those support groups. Sitting in a circle, everyone sharing their stories. It felt like a therapy session, and I ain't much for therapy."

William leaned forward, "Sometimes, facing the demons head-on is the only way to conquer them. Those groups may feel odd at first, but you might find strength in sharing and hearing others."

"I guess I just need to figure out what triggers me to light up. It's like the cravings have a life of their own. I appreciate the advice, William. I don't want to be a slave to these damn cigarettes forever."

"If you ask me, I'd say keep smoking them," Hugh remarked, earning a pointed look from William.

"What?" Hugh met the gaze squarely.

"I need a refreshing shower. I'll make my way back to the room," Hugh conveyed to William as he gracefully rose from his seat.

On the way to his room, Hugh found the corridor outside Soo Ah and Jun Hyuk's room eerily quiet. Hugh approached. He heard from the French girls about the unusual tension between the couple earlier, and curiosity propelled him to investigate. A subtle feeling of unease lingered as he found the door ajar, a thin stream of light seeping through. With cautious steps, he entered, only to be met with emptiness. He scanned the room for any signs of irregularity. The clothes strewn across the bed and the haphazard arrangement of personal items indicated a hasty departure. A faint sound caught his attention—footsteps approaching the door. Panic seized him, and without a second thought, Hugh darted towards the bed and slid underneath, concealing himself in the shadows.

As he crouched in the confined space beneath the bed, the muffled voices of Soo Ah and Jun Hyuk entered the room. Their conversation, rapid and impassioned, unfolded in Korean, a language unfamiliar to Hugh, yet the intensity was palpable. He strained to decipher the emotions threaded into the heated exchange, the rising and falling tones conveying a tale of discord.

The bed above him shuddered slightly as the couple moved around. Hugh's senses heightened, every creak of the floor and hushed whisper amplifying in the confined space beneath.

Soo Ah's voice rose and Jun Hyuk's attempts to pacify her became evident. The language barrier shielded the specifics, but the raw emotions painted a vivid picture of a disagreement spiralling out of control. Hugh strained to catch any clue, his eyes flickering around the dim expanse beneath the bed.

A moment later, the room fell into a heavy silence and the footsteps retreated, fading into the distance. Hugh cautiously emerged from his hiding spot. The room still bore the traces of the clash.

"I need a change of scenery," Hugh declared, and with purposeful steps, he exited the room. Outside, he encountered Jun Hyuk returning.

"Ethan? What brings you here?" Jun Hyuk inquired.

"Oh, I must've taken a wrong turn. This inn, though quaint, can be a bit perplexing," Hugh responded. "Where's Soo Ah?"

"She's in the outdoor seating area. I came back for my jacket," Jun Hyuk explained. "Umm… Would you care to join us for a cup of tea?"

"Of course," Hugh agreed, recognizing Jun Hyuk's courtesy.

The pair strolled towards the outdoor seating area, greeted by a noticeable drop in temperature. Soo Ah sat serenely by the flickering bonfire, enveloped in its warm glow. In their early thirties, Soo Ah and Jun Hyuk formed a striking couple. Soo Ah, a woman of grace, possessed a delicate charm that softened the lines of her face. Her lustrous, jet-black hair cascaded down her shoulders, framing an oval-shaped visage. Her eyes conveyed a warmth that complemented the gentle curve of her lips. Soo Ah's style exuded sophistication, with black trousers and a yellow cardigan that effortlessly blended contemporary fashion with a touch of traditional elegance.

On the other hand, Jun Hyuk exhibited a quiet strength in his physique. His broad shoulders and well-defined features spoke of resilience and determination. With a neatly trimmed beard that outlined a strong jawline, Jun Hyuk carried an air of maturity that complemented his calm demeanour. His attire of a navy-blue sweatshirt and a pair of jeans was a mix of casual and refined, echoing his confident yet approachable personality.

"Good evening, Soo Ah," Hugh greeted, maintaining an air of casualness that masked the probing thoughts beneath. Soo Ah looked up, her eyes revealing a momentary flicker of surprise before settling into a composed expression.

"Good evening, Ethan." Soo Ah offered a polite nod.

"I've been chatting with the French girls," Hugh began, his voice measured. "They mentioned seeing you two on the day Yahia was murdered. Soo Ah, you were in tears, and Jun Hyuk, you were consoling her."

A subtle exchange of glances passed between Soo Ah and Jun Hyuk. The fire's glow reflected in their eyes as they navigated the delicate territory of the conversation.

Soo Ah, with a faint smile, spoke first, "It was just a personal matter. Emotions can be overwhelming sometimes."

Hugh studied their faces, searching for any signs of deception. "Forgive me for prying, but the timing seemed peculiar. Can you shed some light on what happened that day?"

Jun Hyuk sighed, a visible weight on his shoulders. "It was an unexpected call from back home, bringing news that stirred emotions. Soo Ah was understandably upset, and I was trying to comfort her. Unfortunately, the circumstances led to a misunderstanding."

Soo Ah interjected, "We assure you, Ethan, it had nothing to do with Yahia's murder. The timing was purely coincidental."

"The phone lines were down that day," Hugh remarked, "and are still down."

Jun Hyuk exchanged a contemplative look with Soo Ah.

"I sense there's more to the story you shared earlier," Hugh, with a discerning gaze, addressed the couple.

"Listen, the police will be arriving shortly, and you'll have to share your story sooner or later. This isn't Korea; nobody here knows you. Even if everyone learns your tale, they'll return to their homes, and you'll vanish into obscurity," Hugh attempted to persuade them.

Jun Hyuk exhaled a deep breath.

"This is our second marriage. We met back in the summer of 1978 and had admired each other ever since. Our first marriage went smoothly until the news of Soo Ah's pregnancy. Tragically, we lost the baby in the ninth month after Soo Ah fell down the stairs at my parents' house." He held his wife's hand tightly, who reciprocated the gesture.

"I wasn't able to conceive since. I was overwhelmed by grief and decided to end our marriage, but Jun Hyuk did not give up on me."

"I did my best to win her heart back until we remarried last month, and we decided to come here on our honeymoon."

Soo Ah spoke with a quiver in her voice, "Infertility is a deeply personal and sensitive matter. We wanted to deal with it privately, but the emotions overwhelmed us that day. We never expected it to be misconstrued."

Jun Hyuk added, "We don't want our private life becoming a spectacle. We were just trying to come to terms with our own reality."

The flames danced, casting fleeting reflections in Soo Ah's teary eyes. Hugh, recognizing the magnitude of their shared pain, nodded understandingly.

Jun Hyuk offered a nod, "We'll call it a night."

As the couple departed, leaving Hugh in solitary contemplation within the outdoors, his gaze ascended towards the night sky decorated with a tapestry of stars.

"Beautiful," he whispered in hushed tones, almost as if afraid to disturb the serenity of the moment with the resonance of his own voice.

Hugh reclined on the Bedouin style couch, yearning for this fleeting moment to extend into eternity. A soothing interlude unfolded as the turbulent emotions of anger and guilt within him gradually subsided, if only for this ephemeral moment. Succumbing to the soothing ambiance, his eyelids surrendered to the weight of slumber, and Hugh slipped into a profound sleep amid the tranquil desert night.

## **CHAPTER 10: DETECTIVE SALAH**

The following morning, Hugh, who had spent the night under the open sky, was fully awake. He discovered himself snugly wrapped in a thick blanket, a gesture he recognised as William's. Appreciation welled within him for William's discretion in not disturbing his slumber, a departure from William's usual habit.

Hugh ambled towards the reception area, where the assembled tour group awaited. William diligently managed the luggage, packing their belongings and neatly arranging them in the reception area.

"How'd you sleep?" William inquired, his attentiveness evident.

Hugh, wearing a knowing smirk, responded, a hint of fatigue in his expression.

"The police are arriving soon; we're going back to Cairo."

"Good for everyone, yeah? Cairo police did mention they'd arrive within a day, but it ended up taking them two days." Hugh, acknowledging the development nonchalantly, punctuated by a yawn, settled into a chair nearby next to the

French ladies. Hugh observed their composed appearance, both dressed in solemn black. Notably, it was the first occasion since the unsettling incident that Hugh had witnessed Brigitte with makeup.

Brigitte and Jacqueline's luggage stood out amidst the rest. The sophisticated suitcases were crafted from premium hard-shell aluminium with elegant details. Stickers from various destinations were on the exteriors, telling stories of their past adventures and Brigitte's well-maintained leather bag remained faithfully by her side.

William excused himself to check for the anticipated arrival of the authorities.

"Finally, the police are arriving," Jacqueline began, effortlessly initiating the conversation, making it easy for Hugh. He found her very approachable.

Hugh noticed a knitting needle peeking out of Jacqueline's black tote bag, which she carried alongside her luggage.

"Be careful, you might lose something," he remarked, nodding towards the tote bag.

"Oh, my knitting needle," she responded with a smile, tucking it back in. "I do some knitting before bedtime here in Cairo. I have my own business in Paris. Maybe you could support me by buying some when you visit?" she teased.

"Her creations are exquisite," Brigitte finally chimed in.

"Tell me more about this knitting business of yours," Hugh inquired.

"I knit a variety of items; here's my business card."

Hugh's interest heightened as he laid eyes on the business card, three butterflies decorated the card.

"Do you make butterfly-embroidered handkerchiefs?"

"Yes, I do. One of my best-selling items."

"Yahia had a similar handkerchief. Any idea why he had it?"

"Oh, did he? I... I can't say for certain. Interestingly, one of my handkerchiefs seemed to have gone astray during our initial day in Sinai. I must have misplaced it somewhere. Nevertheless, my pieces are frequently either gifted or sold, and I don't keep tabs on where they end up." A hint of uncertainty shadowed her expression.

"These handkerchiefs are quite popular across Europe. Perhaps he ventured there and purchased one, how would we know?" Brigitte interjected.

Hugh, though still intrigued, accepted her response. "Are they?"

"The police have arrived!" Mohammed's announcement resounded as the approaching vehicles drew near the hotel, interrupting their conversation.

Hugh swiftly made his way outside, joining William.

"Detective Ethan! My mate!" A scruffy-looking detective approached Hugh.

The detective's tweed jacket, once deep brown, had faded at the elbows and a loosely knotted tie hung around his neck, hinting at a morning that started early and had yet to ease up. The creases on his beige trousers and worn shoes testified to countless hours spent on the field. William whispered to Hugh that the man was Detective Salah from the Egyptian Police, an old acquaintance of Ethan's. Ethan had been absent since the previous night.

The Egyptian detective got occupied for a moment, issuing instructions to the police and the tour group to board the bus. Returning his attention to Hugh and William, he greeted them cheerfully.

"Oh, William, too! Been ages, hasn't it? Ethan, liking the new hairstyle for winter, eh?"

"Detective Salah, always a pleasure to see you," William greeted.

Hugh gave him a disapproving look but decided to use him to his advantage. Detective Salah didn't seem bothered by Hugh's silence, preoccupied with his own thoughts. He rested his hands on his hips, looking to the ground.

"That earthquake gave us a fright and delayed our arrival. And when we got word from the General Administration of

Tourism & Antiquities Police that an Ankh vanished from the Egyptian museum and was swapped for an identical fake, the situation became a frenzy. Now, we find ourselves collaborating with the TA police on this investigation," Detective Salah said as he used heavy hand gestures.

"Any potential suspects?" Hugh asked.

"None identified yet. The pressure is on, and I can't afford any missteps. As for the Sinai murder, we're instructed to handle foreign suspects with utmost care. Once news of the murder breaks, calls and embassy reps won't stop," he explained, then again got distracted by the police officers assisting the tourists.

"Go on, Detective Salah. We understand you're dealing with a lot," William assured with a nod, acknowledging the detective's demanding responsibilities.

"Not only that, I'm on another case. The White Masked Killer, a lunatic going around murdering women who are exactly twenty-four years old. Thanks to the Ankh disappearance and the chaos in law enforcement, we've had 3 more victims in a matter of days! I've got a lot on my plate, gentlemen," Detective Salah explained before issuing a few instructions in Arabic to his subordinates.

"Interesting case." Hugh said.

"Yes, quite intriguing indeed. But this killer is mine and mine alone!" Detective Salah said in determination.

Hugh forced a smile.

In parting, Detective Salah, maintaining a light-hearted tone, addressed Hugh, "My friend, hop on the bus. I'll catch up with you in Cairo. Don't worry, I'll be the one digging into you two suspects. I'll keep you informed if any new leads emerge." With that, he walked away.

Hugh and William boarded the old bus, both visibly relieved. The worn, cracked leather seats sagged with the weight of years and the air hung heavy with the scent of aged upholstery and traces of diesel fumes that had seeped into the very fabric of the vehicle.

As Hugh sauntered down the aisle, his eyes caught sight of an unoccupied seat beside Daniela, her bag strategically placed to deter anyone from sitting next to her. It seemed to be her discreet method of conveying discomfort. Unperturbed, Hugh picked up her bag and neatly stowed it under the seat, claiming the spot for himself. Daniela, engrossed in a Rubik's cube that defied resolution, shifted her gaze towards him, casting a disdainful glance. Choosing to face the window, she hoped to dissuade any attempts at conversation that Hugh might initiate. Hugh, undeterred, responded with a sardonic smile, even rolling his eyes when he thought she could see his reflection on the window. He aimed to catch Daniela's attention in the window's reflection, attempting to initiate conversation; he found her to be a challenging person to engage with.

"I saw that," she said, shooting a pointed glare at him. "Why choose this seat when there are other empty ones around?"

With nonchalant ease, Hugh took the Rubik's cube from her hand and effortlessly solved it in under a minute. Impressed yet perturbed, she swiftly reclaimed it. Hugh cast a brief glance her way.

"I made countless attempts to crack it during my high school days. It took a while, but I'm sure you'll master it soon," he made-up the high school reference, a part of a history that never belonged to him.

Daniela's face flushed, but she maintained a stoic silence. He offered her a warm smile, fully aware of its persuasive effect, or so he believed.

"It's dreadful what happened to our tour guide. I couldn't help but notice how attentive he was to you," Hugh began, attempting to draw her into conversation.

However, she remained tight-lipped. Growing increasingly impatient, Hugh scrutinized her intently.

"If you know anything that could help, you should share it. He died tragically on that mountain."

"I only witnessed one thing," she asserted, meeting his gaze squarely.

"Please, enlighten me," Hugh pressed on, his attention fully engaged.

"I know you're a detective, but this isn't within your purview. I plan on telling the police everything I know. As for you, you're merely a suspect like the rest of us. How can I be sure it wasn't you?" Daniela gave him a sardonic look.

Hugh replied with a poised smile, concealing the sting he felt inside. Being addressed in such a manner didn't sit well with him. He closed his eyes, leaned his head against the seat, and crossed his arms. Upon reopening his eyes, his gaze voluntarily fixated on Brigitte. Her fingers anxiously fidgeted, the rhythmic tapping of her foot against the floor and the tightening grip on the strap of her leather handbag piqued Hugh's interest.

*All I need now is a good night's sleep.*

\*\*\*\*\*

Hugh straightened his coat, nonchalantly dusting off the remnants of the interrogation room that clung to him. The faded institutional beige of the room's walls left a lingering imprint on his senses, and the subtle aroma of dust hung in the air. As Detective Salah led him out, the dim, flickering light cast intermittent shadows, painting a vivid picture of the cramped and worn investigative space.

In the waiting area, William patiently awaited Hugh's return. The urgency in the Egyptian police's investigation, fuelled by public pressure, hung palpably in the atmosphere. Detective Salah ushered them to his compact office.

Detective's Salah's desk was cluttered with case files and investigative reports. Faded maps adorned the walls, mapping out the intricate web of Cairo's streets and alleys. He asked one of the workers for three cups of tea. As the steaming brew arrived, they sipped in companionable silence.

"Thank goodness the preliminary investigations are concluded. Still trying to figure out this case alongside the TA police on the museum heist," grumbled Detective Salah, audibly sipping his tea, the sound reverberating through the room. Hugh sensed the resonance extending beyond the confines of the police station.

"When can we expect the conclusive results regarding the time of death and the murder weapon?" inquired Hugh.

"Today or tomorrow at the latest," Detective Salah responded.

William nodded in acknowledgment.

"I'm curious about Daniela's interrogation," Hugh added.

"Oh, you won't believe her testimony," Detective Salah exclaimed, leaning forward with a hint of excitement. "So, right after the group checked in on the day of the murder, she was headed to take a walk outside the Sunrise Inn. She said the Hottinger's room was adjacent to the French girls' room, and as she was passing by, she noticed that Jacqueline wasn't there. But Brigitte wasn't alone. So she approached quietly, I guess out of teenager's curiosity? And guess what? Yahia was with Brigitte in the room. They were having some sort of an argument, and Yahia seemed pretty angry. All she heard was Yahia shouting at Brigitte something like, 'I thought you were different. I thought you had changed. What was that letter? Lies?' Then Yahia stormed out of the room and unintentionally collided with Daniela, who dropped her medication on the floor." Detective Salah paused to take a sip of his tea before continuing.

"She said he wasn't concerned about her overhearing and kindly returned some of the medications she dropped. However, Daniela felt embarrassed and fled without heeding his calls to take the rest of her medication."

"So Yahia and Brigitte might have had a prior connection," William contemplated.

"Exactly, my friend."

"Did the interrogations lay a foundation for any suspects?" Hugh asked.

"Everyone seems to have an alibi; it's only a matter of confirming it. Again, Derek and Brigitte seem to have a previous connection with Yahia. We're also looking into the hotel staff."

"A lot of these suspects are hiding something."

"There's nothing I want more than solving all these case," Detective Salah encouraged. "Tell you what… Let's meet up later at my apartment to discuss further findings."

Just as Detective Salah led them out, an impeccably attired police officer intercepted them. His dark brown hair harmonized with his sharp-eyed gaze, bestowing upon him the quintessential appearance of a law enforcement officer. Detective Salah warmly greeted him, following the Egyptian custom of hearty exchanges.

"Our groom!" exclaimed Detective Salah excitedly, eliciting a blush from the officer. "Got the ring yet?"

The officer produced a small box from his pocket, revealing a splendid ring that appeared significantly more valuable than what one might expect from the officer's probable earnings. William appeared taken aback, while Hugh observed with keen interest.

"A gift from my father," the officer smiled.

"Officer Adham Fakhri's dream has finally come true!" Detective Salah's resonant voice shattered Hugh's reverie.

"Mrs Hottinger's ring…" William whispered.

## CHAPTER 11: THE TRAVEL AGENCY

Detective Salah's humble Cairo apartment had a sense of simplicity and modesty. Situated in a quiet neighbourhood, the apartment showcased a blend of traditional Egyptian decor and functional furnishings. Framed family photographs hung on the walls, capturing moments of shared laughter and milestones. A small bookshelf stood in the corner, showcasing a collection of crime novels and investigative works. The curtains, though worn, filtered the soft glow of Cairo's evening lights, forming a warm ambiance over the unassuming living space.

"Your family is truly charming," William remarked as he settled onto the elegant grey couch beside the well-stocked bookshelf.

Detective Salah, with a hint of pride, acknowledged, "They reside down South in a quaint town, while I navigate life here in Cairo." With a warm smile, he offered, "Tea or sodas, perhaps?"

Hugh, gesturing towards the neatly arranged cups of water on the table, responded, "Water should be enough."

"How's the hunt for The White Masked Killer going?" William asked.

"Well, not many leads. It's on my mind twenty-four seven. As you can see, I have two daughters and one son," Detective Salah responded, nodding towards a family photograph with him in the middle, surrounded by his three children. "All I can imagine is, what if any of these murdered women were one of my daughters? I really appreciate your help, gentlemen, on taking the lead on Yahia's case."

"That's what I live for," Hugh said.

"That doesn't mean I'll slack, my friend," Detective Salah chuckled. "Let's go over our clues."

After sharing all findings and details of the interrogations, the conversation shifted to Chef Fakhri's generous gift of Mrs Hottinger's ring to his son, Officer Adham Fakhri. Detective Salah chuckled at the irony, reflecting, "Poor guy. The look in his eyes when he learned of the theft was priceless. He'll accompany us to Sinai tomorrow, and we'll revisit his father's questioning."

William chimed in, "What about the twin brother, Yassine? Any leads on his whereabouts?"

Detective Salah sighed, "According to our records, Yassine served time in prison for armed robbery, was subsequently released, and has been missing for almost a decade, presumably dead."

"Did the police discover anything significant in Yahia's Cairo apartment during their search?" Hugh asked.

"Nothing that would contribute to the ongoing investigation." Detective Salah shook his head. "But I found a very interesting thing peeping out of Derek's pocket during investigation."

"What was it?" William asked.

"A square handkerchief bearing three knitted butterflies in each corner. He claimed he had found it lying on the floor in the study room of the Sunrise Inn."

"A similar handkerchief to the one that was missing from Yahia's bag." Hugh gazed in front of him deeply immersed in his thoughts.

Detective Salah's frustration resonated in his words as he exclaimed, "We discovered a similar handkerchief at the market, and Jacqueline appears to be incessantly crafting these items. It's mind-blowing that she remains oblivious to who is distributing them!" Despite his initial anger, he took a moment to compose himself, inhaling deeply before resuming. "Let's clarify our standing. The initial findings still don't yield a murder weapon. We're eagerly awaiting the detailed autopsy report to narrow down possibilities. No fingerprints were discovered on the body, or at least nothing that matches our database. A handkerchief crafted by Jacqueline was with Yahia, in the market, and with Derek. Derek says he found it lying on the floor, which does not make any sense. Again, this is assuming that her handkerchiefs have become quite popular in Europe. People are buying them, and recently, one of the handkerchiefs she knitted went missing. Yet, this handkerchief wasn't present at the crime scene, and its connection to the murder remains uncertain. Did Yahia lose it in the inn? And let's presume Chef Fakhri stole Mrs Hottinger's ring. No murder weapon, witnesses, or tangible leads. Who would kill the person that everyone loves?" Detective Salah summarised, contemplating the intricate web of details.

"Loved, yet bereft of a family to claim the remains," William uttered with empathy.

"A person cannot be universally loved," Hugh stated, fixing his gaze directly on William.

Detective Salah observed the exchange with a quizzical expression, seemingly unsure of the subtle tension between the two friends. "Anyway, Derek and Brigitte remain key suspects because their connection with Yahia and the unresolved arguments raise red flags. We need to dig deeper into their involvement."

"We should not rule out anyone," Hugh added.

The home phone rang, prompting Detective Salah to hurry over and answer it.

"Detective Salah speaking." He listened intently for five minutes, absorbing the information from the caller before hanging up.

"The autopsy findings have been received. The time of death is estimated between 11:30 p.m. and 1:30 a.m., attributed to blunt force trauma to the head. The suspected murder weapon appears to be gold-plated, as indicated by dried gold paint within the cranial injury. It seems to be a substantial, sharp-edged object, measuring at least 10 centimetres in length."

"Wait a moment, gold paint? The first thing that springs to mind is Soo Ah's gold hairpin," exclaimed William.

"The Korean lady? What could be her motive?" Detective Salah inquired.

"Motive, well..." William pondered for a moment.

"What if the object that fell off Yahia's bag was something Soo Ah desired?" Hugh suggested.

"Why would she want an Egyptian ornament?" William questioned.

"Soo-Ah believes that Egyptian ornaments can bring her good luck and aid in bearing a child," explained Hugh.

"She did appear a bit superstitious. Another suspect to consider," Detective Salah concluded.

"I'd like to head to the crime scene again. I sense we're making progress," Hugh said with a determined gaze.

"Good plan." Detective Salah nodded, acknowledging the strategy.

"Also, I'd like to make a brief stop at the travel agency before we head to Sinai," Hugh said.

"You have the green light from me, my friend."

"Excellent," William added.

\*\*\*\*\*\*

The following morning, accompanied by William, Hugh ventured to the travel agency. The news of Yahia's death had spread, creating a sombre atmosphere. It was evident Yahia had been highly regarded among the agency staff. At his desk, now filled with flowers and photographs, was an absence of family mementoes. The confined space of the agency limited movement for the employees.

Guided by one of the employees, they entered the office of the person they came to meet. A woman, elegantly dressed in black, her posture upright and confident, entered the office after them. Hugh felt a pang of empathy seeing someone so refined working in such cramped quarters. Her desk tag bore the name 'Hala Zahed, General Manager'.

Hugh and William greeted the agency manager with courtesy, and she reciprocated warmly. They introduced themselves, noting that Detective Salah had likely informed her of their arrival. Politely declining her offer of a drink, Hugh gestured to his water bottle, but Hala insisted and promptly asked the office boy for three cups of tea.

"Management has approved the refund for the Sinai trip; it should be ready tomorrow morning. Kindly sign this form," she stated, extending a pen to both Hugh and William.

Hugh swiftly signed the document, and after securing the lid of the pen, he fixed his gaze on the form, repeatedly opening and closing the pen's lid until Hala retrieved the document from him.

"How's the Cleo Hotel? I hope the entire tour group is enjoying their stay there," Hala inquired with a faint smile.

William nodded.

"Detectives, listen. I'm aware you're here about Yahia. I'll cut straight to the chase. He was a gem in our company, no issues with anyone. I couldn't have imagined this is how his life would end," she lamented, her eyes revealing a mix of grief and shock. "I've just returned from a two-week holiday and came back yesterday. I'm originally from Alexandria. I was devastated and the news hit me hard. Yahia wasn't always the exemplary employee you knew him to be. In fact, during his first three months with us, his performance and attitude were less than satisfactory."

"What changed?" Hugh asked, leaning forward slightly in his seat.

Hala leaned back, folding her hands neatly in her lap. "We decided to send him on an internship to Paris, which was fully sponsored by one of our partners," she explained. "It was a last-ditch effort to salvage his potential. And I must say, it worked wonders."

William nodded. "In what way?" he inquired.

Hala's expression softened as she recalled the transformation Yahia underwent.

"When he returned from Paris, he was like a different person," she said, a note of pride in her voice. "He was kinder, more generous, and incredibly hard-working. It was as if the experience had opened his eyes to his true potential. Tourists specifically requested him for their trips."

"Who arranged his internship in Paris?" Hugh inquired with a focused gaze.

"The Louvre," Hala responded, her fingers delicately tapping on the polished surface of the table.

"Can you remember the names of those who managed the internship at the Louvre?" William pressed on.

Hala furrowed her brow, attempting to recall. "I don't quite remember... Bianca, Brenda, someone with a 'B,' I think."

"Brigitte?" Hugh probed.

Recognition dawned on Hala's face. "Oh yes, yes! Ms. Brigitte Dubois," she affirmed.

"Oh, dear God, poor Yahia..." Hala uttered with a tone of sorrow, her vulnerability gradually surfacing. As she spoke, the ambiance of the room seemed to echo the weight of the tragic event.

Sipping her tea, Hala continued, "I can't believe someone could harm such a kind person. Out of disbelief, I even thought I saw someone who looked like him. But it was my mind playing tricks... It definitely wa—"

"When did you see him?" Hugh interrupted.

"Today... It... it was in front of the travel agency... dressed in black, wearing a hoodie, seemed like he was searching for someone... But as I said, my mind was playing tricks..." Hala's voice wavered, revealing the emotional toll the situation had taken on her.

"Has Yahia ever mentioned having a brother?"

"A brother? No, he always said that he was an only child…"

Hugh exchanged a glance with William when Hala's phone rang abruptly. After answering and exchanging pleasantries with Detective Salah, she handed the phone to Hugh.

"Listen carefully. A handful of onlookers spotted Yahia earlier today in a supermarket adjacent to the travel agency."

"Only that it isn't Yahia. We need to find Yassine as soon as possible; he's lingering around."

"Oh, we do. A salary boost is long overdue."

"Have they completed the analysis of the CCTV footage from the Cleo Hotel?"

"It's still in progress. Expect the results by the time we return from Sinai. You know what? We're lucky that the Cleo Hotel has CCTV cameras installed; it's probably the first hotel in Cairo to do so. That's why I like rich people places, make things easy for me. Anyway, I'm making my way to the travel agency now; be prepared, my friend."

Hugh disconnected the call, a sense of urgency written across his face.

"We must leave," Hugh rose from his seat.

"If you happen to spot Yahia, kindly notify Detective Salah at once," William said, moving decisively towards the exit with Hugh.

"B-but..." Hala stammered, bewildered.

"Do as he says," urged Hugh as he slammed the door behind him.

## **CHAPTER 12: SINAI AGAIN**

"Welcome back!" Mohammed greeted with genuine enthusiasm, a rare occurrence in the quiet aftermath of recent events.

William reciprocated the warmth, patting Mohammed on the shoulder. "Good to see you, lad."

The inn, once bustling with activity, now bore the weight of its tarnished reputation.

"I'm supposed to leave tomorrow evening. The inn's reputation is in tatters after the incident. I must await upper management's decision on reopening," Mohammed explained, his tone reflecting the uncertainty shrouding the inn's future.

Detective Salah, seated at the reception desk, indulged in local biscuits. Leaning back, he wiped away the crumbs, his actions deliberate and unhurried.

"We're here to see Chef Fakhri," he announced, initiating the purpose of their visit.

"He's in the kitchen preparing our dinner, as he has been doing since the shutdown of the inn," Mohammed replied, his voice tinged with a mix of hospitality and resignation.

"Let's not startle him with an interrogation trio. I'll accompany Officer Fakhri to the kitchen. You two can engage with Mohammed here," Hugh suggested, subtly guiding Officer Adham Fakhri towards the kitchen, without affording a moment for the two other men to respond.

"I agree," Adham said.

"Oh, Detective Ethan's ego rearing its head again," Detective Salah chuckled, savouring the last few bites of the biscuits.

William nodded in agreement. He was the only one who knew that the ego in question belonged to Hugh and not Ethan.

Hugh noticed officer Adham Fakhri's hesitation as he approached the quaint kitchen of the Sunrise Inn where his father, Chef Fakhri, devoted his life to culinary excellence. It had been months since they last met, and the conflicting emotions within him churned like a stormy sea. The aroma of spices and sizzling delicacies wafted through the air as he pushed open the door, revealing his father, with a white apron wrapped around his waist, looking up from the stove. His eyes lit up with genuine joy at the sight of his son. "Adham! My boy!" he exclaimed, wiping his hands on a kitchen towel before embracing his son.

Adham, however, remained stiff in the embrace, a complex mixture of emotions clouding his face. "It's been a while, Father," he replied, his voice guarded.

Chef Fakhri appeared to have noticed the tension but chose to brush it aside, leading Adham to a corner table. "Sit, sit! I've been waiting for this day. How have you been?"

Hugh positioned himself by the door, observing the unfolding conversation with rapt attention. Leaning casually against the wall, one foot placed slightly behind the other, he watched in suspense.

Adham took a deep breath, deciding to address the matter that had been gnawing at him. "Father, I've heard things. About a stolen ring. Mrs Hottinger's ring, the one you sent to me, claiming to have purchased it with your hard-earned money for my bride?"

Chef Fakhri's jovial expression faltered momentarily, and he averted his gaze. "Ah, Adham, my boy, it's... it's not what you think. I... I did not steal it."

"How is it, then, that you had it?"

"It was... it was... the... the teenage girl..."

"Daniela gave it to you? Why?" Hugh interrupted.

"I've witnessed her indulging in a spliff; it is very accessible here in Sinai. She probably got it from one of the Bedouin groups near the supermarket close by and, well, she suggested I could take the ring if I didn't tell her father and aunt about it. However, being a father myself, I felt the need to discuss it with the Hottingers. They, in turn, permitted me to keep it but urged me to refrain from disclosing the fact that Daniela was the source, aiming to spare themselves any potential embarrassment," Chef Fakhri revealed with a conflicted expression on his face.

Adham's eyes narrowed. "Keep it? Father, you can't accept it. I can't accept this ring, and we need to return it to the owner."

Chef Fakhri sighed, a weariness settling in his eyes. "I... I didn't mean for it to cause trouble, Son. I wanted the best for you."

As the father and son grappled with their moral dilemma, the door chimed, and Detective Salah entered with William.

"So, what's going on?" Detective Salah inquired, sensing the tension.

Adham explained the situation, detailing his concerns about the ring. Chef Fakhri defended himself, emphasizing that Daniela had gifted it to him.

William interjected, "Returning the ring is the right thing to do, Chef Fakhri."

Chef Fakhri hesitated, his eyes flickering with uncertainty. "I will return it to the Hottinger's myself; don't worry."

"Glad we cleared this one up. Daniela seems to be quite a source of frustration for her family," Detective Salah remarked.

"Dr Harrington and I shall proceed to the crime scene to ensure we haven't overlooked any crucial elements." The flickering fluorescent lights in the kitchen cast eerie shadows on the floor, mirroring the uncertainty that clouded Hugh's mind.

"Very well. I shall look around the inn and try to establish contact with the police station, looking for any available updates," Detective Salah affirmed.

The narrow mountain path wound its way through the rugged terrain as Hugh and William embarked on their quest for clues. The jagged rocks and scattered pebbles crunched beneath their boots, creating a symphony of natural sounds. The wind whispered through the sparse shrubs, carrying the scent of dry earth and adventure.

"Keep an eye out, Doctor. We might stumble upon something significant," Hugh suggested, his keen eyes scanning the rocky landscape.

As they ascended, the panoramic view of the Sinai landscape unfolded before them, a vast expanse of untamed beauty. The distant echoes of wildlife reverberated through the air, providing a backdrop to their investigative journey.

"What exactly are we looking for?" William inquired, adjusting his tie.

"Anything unusual. Something out of place. Something we might have missed," Hugh replied, stooping to examine a cluster of rocks.

Their search led them to a secluded area, away from the beaten path and leading to the inn. William spotted a peculiar indentation in the soil and gestured towards it.

"Hugh, take a look at this."

Bending down, Hugh scrutinized the ground. The imprint resembled a shallow depression, distinct from the natural irregularities of the rocky surface. He reached into his pocket and pulled out a pair of gloves, preparing to unearth the mystery beneath the soil.

After a few careful movements, the pair discovered a small, black crystal—an unexpected discovery in the harsh wilderness. Hugh examined the crystal in his hand.

"Faux crystal," Hugh said.

"How do you know that?"

"Authentic crystals from nature have a coolness to the touch and a weightiness. This one lacks both," Hugh said, securing the faux crystal in an evidence bag.

Before they could delve into the implications of their find, Mohammed appeared on the rocky path, panting with urgency.

"Detectives! We found something at the inn," Mohammed exclaimed, his eyes wide with anticipation.

The duo followed Mohammed back down the mountain, retracing their steps. Upon reaching the inn, they were ushered towards the shared bathroom, where the atmosphere hummed with anticipation.

"What have you found?" Hugh inquired as they entered.

Mohammed pointed towards a blocked drain, and a maintenance worker was diligently working to clear the obstruction.

"We found this while fixing the blockage. Thought you should know," Mohammed explained, his eyes reflecting a mix of concern and curiosity.

The worker extracted a clump of debris, revealing a small, black faux crystal snuggled within.

"Identical to the crystal we discovered by the mountain." Hugh cradled it in his hand, subjecting it to a thorough inspection and continued. "Did you see anyone use the shared bathroom on the day of the murder?"

"I mean, no one in particular; most of the guests used it."

Detective Salah burst into the bathroom unannounced. "I've discovered traces of blood on the exterior of the French ladies' room window."

"Things are taking an interesting turn," Hugh said.

"They are. I've liaised with the police department; the CCTV footage will be at our disposal by noon tomorrow." He looked around and then continued, "Now, would someone be so kind as to brief me on the situation?"

"We'll bring you up to speed on our journey to Cairo. Once there, drop me off at Yahia's apartment," Hugh responded, shifting his attention to William. "I'd rather tackle this matter solo."

"Then, I'll try to gather more information by conducting further interrogations with both Soo Ah, Derek, and the French ladies," William said.

"Good! Let's go," Detective Salah instructed as he took the lead out of the bathroom. Hugh winced, his hand reaching for his head as a sharp headache surged through him.

"No..." Hugh murmured under his breath. He glanced briefly at William, his eyes different.

"Ethan? No, it isn't Ethan…" William whispered.

But the eyes filled with anger, determination, and a thirst for justice, were back.

"It's still me," Hugh said, his voice weaker.

"That wasn't Eth…" William murmured to himself.

"My friends! What's all this whispering about? No time for small talk. We still need to get Ethan to Yahia's apartment and I need to head to the station for more leads on the White Masked Killer!" Detective Salah yelled loudly.

## CHAPTER 13: ONE COLD WINTER

**Winter 1978**

It was a chilly morning, the brisk air biting at Ethan's cheeks. He warmed his hands by exhaling into them and then slipped on his leather gloves. The train station bustled with people, eagerly awaiting the arrivals and departures of their loved ones. The track noises and bell chimes echoed like heartfelt greetings and farewells. Ethan's face lit up upon spotting a familiar figure he had awaited. The man reciprocated with a smile, followed by a warm hug and a pat on the shoulder.

"William, I've missed you over the past month," Ethan greeted.

"I hope my absence wasn't too difficult for you," replied William.

Ethan nodded. "How was Bordeaux? Did you manage to settle things with your cousin for the agreed amount?"

"I certainly did," William smiled. "I suppose I've always been the family favourite."

They both laughed.

"What do you plan to do with all that money then?" Ethan inquired as they strolled out of the port.

"Let's just say it's for emergencies," William replied. As they walked, a homeless boy in a tattered coat, clutching a few coins collected from passers-by, accidentally bumped into Ethan.

"Mind where you're going, lad," William scolded the thirteen-year-old.

"Sorry, Sir, my apologies," the boy quickly responded, retrieving the coins that had fallen. Ethan bent down to assist the boy, reaching for the coins on the ground.

"Come on, William, it couldn't be his fault entirely." Ethan winked at the boy, who smiled shyly. He picked up a pocket watch from the floor, seemingly stolen.

"Is this yours?" A sudden headache struck Ethan. "No, Hugh, not now." He held his head tightly.

"Ethan… Ethan…" William supported him to keep his balance.

"Sir, are you okay?" the little boy asked as he grabbed the pocket watch from Ethan's hand. Ethan remained in pain on the floor.

"Kid, you can leave now," William instructed the boy, who nodded and left quickly, relieved not to be questioned any further.

William helped Ethan get back on his feet.

"That's not the way to talk to a little child," Ethan said after the pain subsided.

"Hugh? You aren't exactly the best person to take social advice from," William replied sarcastically, not particularly pleased to encounter Hugh as soon as he arrived in London.

"Hugh? I'm afraid you are mistaken. Call me Charles."

"Charles...?" William exclaimed in shock.

Charles sensed William's surprise, a silent tension between them as they walked. It was as if William hadn't expected another personality, Charles, to surface so soon—if at all. Charles could feel the weight of William's gaze, heavy with questions and concern. Was there a specific trigger that brought Charles forth? Charles wondered what William might be thinking, what theories were forming behind those thoughtful eyes.

As Charles took the lead, guiding them silently around the train station, he was acutely aware of the careful observation from William. Charles moved with an odd slowness, an incongruity that made him seem like an old man caught in a younger man's existence. His posture, his gait—all of it seemed borrowed from another time, another life. Then, as if breaking free from an internal reverie, Charles spoke, his voice slicing through the quiet, carrying the weight of years he hadn't lived.

"What's your name?"

"Me? I'm... Uh... William... William Harrington," William replied nervously. "Actually, I'm the doctor responsible for the person you just put to sleep, Ethan?"

Charles laughed. "You mean the one who kept an eighty-three-year-old man asleep all these years?" He rubbed his wrists and continued. "So, Ethan is his name? I see that no one respects their elders nowadays."

William remained silent.

"So, William, let us have a snack."

Later, after leaving the train station, William followed Charles as he led the way to St. James Park. The park nestled beside a serene lake, with numerous benches inviting pedestrians to rest and soak in the tranquil atmosphere. However, that morning was unusually cold, with only a few people on the benches. An elderly lady selling chestnuts wandered around, hoping to find someone willing to buy these warm snacks. Charles approached the old lady, dressed in rugged clothes.

"I'll have one," Charles said, searching for any coins in Ethan's pockets. Then, he turned to William, who seemed uneasy. "Make it two, please," Charles added, addressing the old lady. They both received the wrapped chestnuts and William murmured a thank you. Charles paused, seemingly noticing the bread the old lady was selling.

"I'll take a pack of those too; these pigeons must be starving in this harsh weather," Charles remarked. The old lady smiled warmly and said, "You're a kind, handsome young man."

Charles laughed heartily, "An old man like me can't possibly be handsome and young." He walked away with William, who huffed sarcastically, overhearing the old lady muttering to herself in surprise, "And humble, too."

For William, sorting his grandmother's inheritance in Bordeaux made those warm chestnuts all the more enjoyable. He appreciated Charles' gesture but remained cautious around this enigmatic new presence. He observed the elderly man feeding breadcrumbs to the park's pigeons as they stopped next to the lake's rail.

"What a serene morning," remarked Charles, gazing at the tranquil lake.

"I'm at a loss for words."

"Speak your mind; share your thoughts."

A contemplative silence enveloped them for a moment.

"Is life just black or white?" William pondered aloud.

"Life can be whatever you make of it," Charles replied, meeting William's gaze, who seemed a touch unsettled by the response. "You choose your path."

"But what if taking that path means hiding the truth to protect the ones you care for the most?" William asked, refraining from taking another chestnut.

"Shouldn't they understand the truth?" Charles smiled. William had much to express but remained silent. "Life's complexities are hard to unravel," Charles said, facing the lake and resting his elbows on the rail.

"Doing what's right doesn't mean giving up on someone." Watching the few people pass through the park, Charles spoke gently. "Courage. It takes courage."

For the first time, William felt like the one needing guidance. Charles seemed to comprehend him, and William decided that Charles embodied the wisdom within Ethan. Charles knew William didn't want him to fade away; he'd wanted to know more about him. Yet, Charles vanished without a word, leaving William with void and endless thoughts. It was the first and last time Charles appeared before him.

## CHAPTER 14: YAHIA'S APARTMENT

Hugh inserted the key into the door's aperture, the metallic clink resonating in the quietude that enveloped the corridor. With a gentle turn, he unlocked the door, which swung open on protesting hinges, releasing a subtle but persistent squeak that reverberated through the hushed atmosphere.

He stepped into Yahia's modest Cairo apartment, a space that echoed simplicity and a touch of melancholy. The faded wallpaper hinted at years of wear, bearing the scars of a life lived with its fair share of struggles. The furniture, though functional, showed signs of age.

The living room welcomed him with a blue worn-out couch, its cushions showing the impressions of countless sittings. A small rectangular coffee table stood in the centre, bearing a few scattered magazines and a clear mug with a dried-out teabag. The muted colours of the room dominated with earthy browns and subdued greens. Yahia's personal touches were evident in the scattered nature paintings on the walls.

As Hugh made his way towards the bedroom, he noted the simple yet functional kitchen. The shelves held an assortment of basic ingredients, and a small dining table stood nearby, suggesting solitary meals in quiet contemplation. The window, decorated with slightly frayed curtains, allowed a sliver of Cairo's bustling life to filter into the apartment.

Entering Yahia's bedroom, Hugh couldn't help but feel a sense of intrusion into the personal sphere of the deceased. The bed, neatly made, showed a person who sought solace in routine. A small desk near the window held notebooks filled with Yahia's planned itineraries for tourists. On the bedroom wall, more paintings, all of Saint Catherine Mountain, were placed. The wardrobe, with its doors slightly ajar, revealed a modest collection of clothes.

As he immersed himself in Yahia's world, Hugh felt an increasing connection to the man who had met a heart-breaking end.

"What are these feelings? Is it Ethan who's sensing this?"

He approached the mirror positioned beside the wardrobe, fixing his gaze upon his reflection with a determined intensity in his eyes.

"Ethan, come out." His impatience was evident in the furrowed brows and the tapping of his fingers against an imaginary surface.

"Come out," Hugh repeated, his voice now louder.

He stared at his reflection, trying to find Ethan within him. He could feel him closer.

"Where are you? Reveal yourself!"

Across from him on the mirror reflection, the primary persona, Ethan, stood defensively, guarded, and wary. The internal dialogue began, the echoes of their mental dual reverberating through the recesses of Hugh's consciousness. Hugh, the stern and determined detective, glared at Ethan with accusatory eyes.

"Haven't you run away enough, Ethan? Your cowardice has haunted us for far too long," Hugh spat, his words cutting through the internal silence.

"What do you want from me?" Ethan said, the usual vibrancy in his gaze faded.

Hugh smirked sarcastically and stared directly at his own reflection—Ethan's reflection.

"Hugh, you don't understand. Some things are best left buried. I can't handle it."

"Don't play the victim. Running away from your past won't change anything," retorted Hugh, frustration etching his features.

"You always blame me for everything," Ethan muttered, his gaze avoiding Hugh's intense stare.

"This isn't about blame; it's about finding justice. For Yahia, for your parents," Hugh asserted, his resolve unwavering.

As the argument intensified, fragments of memories flickered in the mental space, bringing forth glimpses of a painful past that Ethan had fought so hard to conceal. The room transformed, reflecting the shifting emotions within Ethan's psyche. Ethan started to shiver.

"Why are you running away from solving your parents' murder? Your parents needed you, but you chose to escape," accused Hugh, reopening a long-forgotten wound.

Ethan's eyes betrayed a mix of sorrow and defensiveness. "I can't bear the weight of it all. That's the only way to survive."

Hugh, unyielding in his pursuit of truth, countered, "Surviving isn't an excuse for abandoning those who depend on you. You left them alone, vulnerable."

Ethan's mental landscape trembled with the echoes of suppressed memories. The room, once serene, now crackled with an electrifying tension, mirroring the internal strife. Hugh persisted, his determination cutting through the chaos.

"Do not run away from Yahia's murder, Ethan. We can't change the past, but we can uncover the truth and bring justice," Hugh implored, a beacon of logic amidst the tumult.

In the depths of Ethan's mind, the battle waged on—a clash between the detective seeking answers and the wounded soul yearning for protection. The unresolved conflict lingered, leaving Ethan torn between the desire for closure and the fear of confronting the ghosts of his past.

"We've travelled this path before. I have no desire to unravel murders, nor do I yearn for the pursuit of justice. Let the investigators handle it. My aspiration is a peaceful existence, distanced from all this, distanced from you." Ethan sighed, his exhalation carrying with it the weariness of someone who sought solace amidst the chaos.

"You will never destroy my existence, Ethan. I shall persist, an indelible presence until you choose to collaborate with me." Hugh smirked at his reflection, a wily confidence in his gaze.

"I yearn to rid myself of you," Ethan exclaimed.

"If you genuinely want to cast me aside, then align your efforts with mine."

"In working alongside you, I'd be compelled to confront my own demons."

"We can't solve Yahia's murder without facing our own demons, let alone any crime. You've hidden behind this façade for too long," Hugh insisted, his voice unwavering.

Ethan looked down, grappling with the internal turmoil. "I just want to forget."

"We're a detective…"

"*You're* a detective! I am a chef!"

"Ethan Abbott Private Investigation Office?" Hugh mocked, gesturing with his hand towards an imaginary sign with a sardonic smile. "Your name is plastered on it."

"You made me do it!"

"I will compel you to do many more things if you continue to resist. I always win, Ethan."

Ethan fell silent, his fists clenched.

"I'll ensure your victories won't last," Ethan muttered defiantly.

"We owe it to ourselves and to those who rely on us. Let me access your memories of Egypt," Hugh retorted, his gaze unyielding.

As the mental struggle continued, memories flashed before Ethan's eyes—the loss of his parents, the trauma that had led to the creation of Hugh as a protective shield. The room seemed to close in on him, infused with the weight of unresolved issues.

"I can't do this alone. I need access to those memories, Ethan. We need to piece together the puzzle and find justice for Yahia," Hugh urged, his tone less harsh but still firm.

Ethan hesitated, his internal conflict palpable. "Fine, but only for Yahia."

As the sharp tendrils of agony seized control, Hugh clutched his temples in a desperate attempt to quell the storm inside his head. He fell to the ground. A relentless ache, pulsating with every beat of his heart, sent shockwaves of torment through his entire being.

His breaths became shallow, and the world around Hugh blurred, as if a veil had descended over his senses, distorting reality into a disorienting kaleidoscope of hues.

Every attempt to move sent ripples of anguish through his skull, rendering him momentarily paralyzed. The very act of opening his eyes to the hazy light felt like an affront to his fragile state, as the seconds stretched into an eternity.

Hugh, caught in the grip of this unseen assailant, longed for a pardon—for the pain to ebb away and release him from its cruel clutches.

Summoning every ounce of strength, Hugh heaved himself upright from the floor. As he surveyed the confines of Yahia's bedroom, a flood of memories from Ethan's sojourn in Cairo inundated his consciousness. His gaze gravitated towards the array of paintings on the walls, each one meticulously arranged in haphazard elegance. The artworks depicted the majestic Saint Catherine Mountain, the very summit that bore witness to Yahia's tragic demise.

"My favourite part is...." Hugh mused, ambling towards the window adjacent to the desk, "when the cool breeze gently sweeps over the mountain; it's enchanting, like it's safeguarding delightful memories beneath its airy touch."

Hugh unlatched the window, allowing the gust of wind to sweep into the room.

"The wind gushing towards the left... cold breeze sweeps over the mountain..."

Hugh trailed off, following the course of the air. It guided him to the most vibrant painting among them all, depicting the sunset on Saint Catherine. Carefully, he removed the painting from the wall, scrutinizing the empty space behind it.

Opening the frame, he continued Yahia's words from Ethan's memory, "Like it is safeguarding delightful memories beneath its airy touch..."

He discovered a paper ripped from a journal and an envelope. Hugh delved into the written words of the Journal Entry before him.

*Journal Entry - Paris Adventure & New Me*

*Amidst the complexities of our lives, journaling remains my sanctuary, keeping me tethered to sanity.*

*Paris proved to be a magical escapade, enchanting me with its irresistible allure. The Eiffel Tower captivated my attention like a powerful magnet.*

*The true highlight of the trip, however, was the companionship of Yassine. Despite his stressful work at the travel agency and the challenges of his business matters in France, this journey served as his escape from a life he wished to leave behind permanently. Gratefully, I convinced him to bring me along, offering me a dream opportunity to quench my unyielding thirst for history.*

*As we sat on a bench near the Eiffel Tower, I couldn't help but wonder how we, as brothers, let alone twin brothers, ended up on such different paths. Yassine, acknowledging the challenges of his work and life, shared a moment of warmth with me. I dared to question why he couldn't be the lucky twin, but his response was a kind smile and a declaration that he indeed was the fortunate one. According to him, it was me who had the misfortune of having a brother like him.*

*My brother is burdened by his history as an ex-convict involved in illegal activities and the drug trade. He can't seem to get over the shattered career prospects and thinks it is akin to a crumpled paper tossed away, never to be smoothed out again. I will never regret letting him use my identity post-prison, especially after his job searches proved futile, and change seemed elusive. Together, we erased Yassine and lived as one, Yahia.*

*I sometimes struggle to understand why Yassine believes Egypt has been unjust to him when it is his choices that have shaped his life.*

*But what he told me today will finally make both our lives better. I will finally leave our small town and my teaching career at the local school and work for the travel agency. I will take his place; everyone thinks he is Yahia anyways. He said that he secured a job here in Paris at the Louvre and it is time for him to pay me back for all the years I stood by him.*

*Yassine's commitment to turning his life around fills me with pride, and he embarks on a fresh start in France.*

*As for me, my love for Egypt remains unwavering, a sentiment I hold close to my heart. Yet, the prospect of visiting Yassine every summer in Paris fills me with anticipation and excitement.*

*This journal entry stands out as a personal favourite, sharing incredible news for both Yassine and me.*

*It's truly uplifting to sign off with my newfound job title.*

*The Tour Guide*

Hugh deftly folded the paper, diverting his attention to the delicate task of handling the accompanying envelope. It was elegantly sealed with three small butterflies at the tip and delicate handwriting that read, "My dearest Yahia." Intrigued, Hugh eagerly unsealed it. He found a photograph of Yahia, standing alongside his brother and a young lady with a broad smile, her brown hair harmonizing with her eyes.

"Brigitte..." Hugh turned the photograph around, revealing the inscription.

"April 1982. Paris, France."

Hugh's eyes moved across the letter.

*"My Dearest Yahia,*

*The past two weeks have been the best in my life. I'm sorry... I'm not sure if an apology is enough. But meeting someone like you made me rethink my life choices. Money shouldn't determine one's values.*

*Use this brown leather bag. I bought it from a shop near my house; I have one, too. Let it symbolise our flourishing career as tour guides...*

*Once again... I am deeply sorry...*

*When I visit Egypt, I would appreciate it if you could pretend we haven't met before. It would give us the opportunity to become acquainted for the first time... once again.*

*Until the day you see the real me...*

*Always remember,*

*Brigitte..."*

## CHAPTER 15: CLEO HOTEL

The next morning, Hugh, William, and Detective Salah found themselves huddled in the low-lit surveillance room of the police station; eyes fixed on the grainy footage playing across the array of monitors. The flickering glow illuminated their faces, mirroring the tension that permeated the room.

On the screen, the CCTV captured the corridors of Cleo Hotel, where an enigmatic altercation occurred. Yahia, the once-vibrant tour guide, was now portrayed in a different light—engaged in a heated exchange with an unseen adversary. The intensity of the argument was palpable, the muted video betraying the audio urgency of the confrontation.

Hugh leaned forward, squinting at the screen, attempting to discern any detail that might provide a clue. The absence of the other participant in the altercation left an unsettling void, shrouding the mystery in shadows. Hugh noted pills scattering across the floor during the confrontation.

Hugh replayed the footage, dissecting each frame for potential clues.

"It's like a scene from a noir film," mused William, his academic curiosity piqued.

Detective Salah nodded in agreement, his keen gaze meticulously scrutinizing every detail. "Were all members of the tour group lodged on the same floor?"

"Yes, we were all on the same floor," William responded. "Have you had the chance to witness the grandeur of the Cleo Hotel? It's massive, a hundred rooms on each floor."

"Lucky for you to stay there. Perhaps one day I'll have the opportunity," Detective Salah remarked with a laugh. "Our priority is to unravel Yahia's altercation and the significance of these pills. It's interesting that the altercation occurred here in Cairo rather than in Sinai. If the person in that footage is our suspect, it suggests he's been holding a grudge for some time."

Hugh and William nodded in agreement.

"Yahia's burial took place today here in Cairo, with no family present, only colleagues and some people from his town." Detective Salah continued.

"Yassine might make a visit to his brother once the eyes are no longer watching," Hugh remarked.

"Unless, of course, he's the one who desired his death from the start," William said.

"The letters you stumbled upon, my friend, provide us with more reason to believe it's his brother. Yassine was, after all, a troublemaker, a convict entangled in drugs, theft, and the like," Detective Salah remarked.

"We need to figure out the motive," Hugh asserted.

"He's likely back on drugs, weary of his brother's constant admonishing, and decided to get rid of him. Some people detest nagging, trust me; I've been in homicide for so long," Detective Salah said.

Hugh and William fell into a contemplative silence, engrossed in their thoughts.

"What about the interrogations you did while I was in Yahia's apartment?" Hugh asked William.

"Well, there's no new information from Soo Ah; she appears quite steadfast in her account. The French ladies have nothing new to add either, sticking to their original story. Derek remains characteristically quiet, maintaining the narrative he provided earlier. However, Jacqueline mentioned something intriguing. She claims to have sensed that someone is following her at the Cleo Hotel."

"Following her? Oh, dear, the intricacies of this situation are giving me a headache," Detective Salah exclaimed.

"Who could it be?" Hugh inquired.

"I think I know who it might be. I'll delve into it and get to the bottom of things," William said.

"I've also summoned Chef Fakhri and Mohammed for additional questioning," Detective Salah added.

"Very well. Let's return to the hotel. I need to scrutinize this corridor. The timestamp on the CCTV footage indicates it occurred during breakfast before we head to Saint Catherine; let's see if someone observed or overheard something," Hugh declared, rising from his chair.

"Let's proceed," William responded.

"It's preferable for you two to wait in the hotel lobby, so we don't cause a commotion," Hugh suggested.

"We're the police; we can search wherever we want," Detective Salah asserted.

"Well, it's best not to draw attention to us; the killer might be lurking nearby," Hugh offered as an excuse, secretly wanting to investigate alone.

"Oh well…" William acquiesced.

Intrigue lingered in the air as Hugh navigated through the labyrinthine corridors of the Cleo Hotel towards the site of the mysterious CCTV altercation. The hushed whispers of the hotel cleaners echoed in the background. Observing a cleaning housekeeper attempting to enter a room in the corridor, he intercepted her before she could proceed.

With a courteous nod, Hugh delicately inquired about their cleaning schedule. "How frequently do you tend to these corridors?"

The diligent cleaner, her face bearing traces of weariness, responded, "Every day, Sir. We ensure everything is immaculate for the guests."

"How many cleaners have been assigned to this floor in the past two weeks?"

She sighed, "My colleague, Aya, underwent an appendectomy, and I've been shouldering the cleaning responsibilities for this floor alone. My back is killing me."

"Managing all hundred rooms alone?"

"Well, thankfully, only thirty of them are currently occupied."

"Have you come across anything out of the ordinary in the past two weeks on this floor?"

"Out of the ordinary? No, nothing really."

"Keep me informed if you happen to discover anything. I'm in room 312."

The cleaner shrugged in confusion and proceeded to open the door, embarking on her cleaning duties.

Hugh pressed on down the corridor, his observant eyes scouring for any overlooked hints. The carpet beneath his feet wove a tapestry of muted patterns and the air carried the robust scent of cleaning supplies.

Upon arriving at the precise location where the CCTV had captured Yahia's confrontation, Hugh crouched down, his fingers delicately skimming the polished surface of the sideboard at the corridor's conclusion.

While examining beneath the sideboard, Hugh's fingertips encountered a lone pill. He scrutinized it closely, a solitary piece of the puzzle that had managed to evade the diligent efforts of the hotel cleaners in their daily routines.

"Not quite spotless, I see," Hugh remarked sarcastically.

Intrigued, Hugh persisted in his exploration, his fingertips probing for more beneath the sideboard. For a few minutes, it was only dust and a scattering of particles, but then, his eyes widened as he felt something distinct. Retracting his hand, he discovered a slightly worn black tassel. Empowered by this newfound evidence, Hugh rose from his crouched position and proceeded to the lobby to rendezvous with the other two detectives.

The lobby, typically abuzz with activity, was unusually serene. Detective Salah and William engaged in a light-hearted discussion about the distinctions between Egyptian and English cats when Hugh interjected.

"Detective Salah, kindly request the police station to conduct tests on these pills and determine their composition."

"A bit more hands-on, I see. Anything else uncovered?"

"Not at the moment."

"Very well. I'll make my way to the police station and join you later after dinner at this very spot."

Detective Salah departed, leaving the two friends alone in the lobby.

"You've found something, haven't you?" William inquired.

"I'm on the verge of unravelling it all. I can't afford to lose focus now. Remember, Dr Harrington, I'm the one funding your salary," Hugh retorted.

"Your pay check isn't my primary concern, Hugh. There are more significant matters at hand."

"What's your primary concern? Let me give a guess… Ethan?" Hugh smiled sarcastically.

"I appreciate your unique charm, Hugh. You may be obnoxious, but we all harbour an unsightly side."

Though Hugh sensed the underlying passive-aggressiveness, he refused to let anyone gain the upper hand.

"I'll head to my room for a nap until dinner," William declared. "I've known you long enough to realise you won't share your findings with me."

Hugh paid little heed; solitude was his desire. Seated in the chair, he delved into profound contemplation, assembling the puzzle pieces in his mind, delving into Ethan's memories, and sifting through every piece of evidence at his disposal. Hours and hours drifted by; his mind entangled with thoughts of everything around him and everyone inside him. His musings persisted until William nudged him and interrupted his thoughts.

"Are you serious? It's been five hours since I left you. You've been sitting here all this time?"

"I have no time. I need to find the killer."

"You will."

"How was your long nap?" Hugh asked.

"Well, I didn't really go for a nap. I trailed Jacqueline around the hotel, and in doing so, I found her stalker," William disclosed.

"You did? Who is it?"

"The same person who pilfered her handkerchief: Derek."

"I sensed there was something amiss with that fellow."

"I confronted him. He was peering through her window on the day of the murder, entered the room, and took one of her handkerchiefs. Then, upon hearing footsteps, he exited through the window, injuring the palm of his hand on the windowsill. This explains the blood Detective Salah discovered on the window."

"So, it wasn't a mishap in the room. That explains the empty trash in the architects' room."

"The jealousy from Yahia, the way he eyed Jacqueline, his social awkwardness, an inability to cope with rejection from his father's side, and a tendency to attribute his problems to someone else's fault, all of it gives it away."

"Quite the psychologist you are; I give you that. Will you tell Jacqueline?"

"I told him he should be glad that it was me who uncovered the truth, and he's lucky Jacqueline is departing tomorrow, ensuring they won't cross paths for good."

"So, you gave him some leniency?"

"For now."

"When do we get the lab report on the pill? I know I am right."

"Right about what?"

Hugh remained silent.

"Well, Detective Salah is on his way here with the results," William said.

Hugh nodded.

"Come on, let's head to the terrace. The tour group is having one last dinner before everyone heads back home tomorrow."

"Bill's on me. I'd like to treat everyone to this final meal." Hugh said.

The dinner lounge of the Cleo Hotel buzzed with locals mingling with tourists. Plush furnishings, tastefully arranged, beckoned guests to unwind and appreciate the Nile River's majestic view through the expansive windows. Hugh and William could smell the aroma of freshly brewed coffee, and the tantalizing scent of various delicacies wafted through the air. The buffet showcased Egyptian delights that harmoniously shared the stage with international offerings. The terrace, overlooking the meandering Nile, provided a picturesque setting for the tour group to indulge in a leisurely dinner, enjoying the cold breeze and the rhythmic flow of the river below.

Hugh, William, Mike, Jake, Derek, Jun Hyuk, Brigitte, Jaqueline, Mrs Hottinger, Mr Hottinger, and Daniela gathered around a lavishly adorned table with vibrant Egyptian tablecloths. The air was infused with the aromatic allure of Egyptian delicacies, a tempting fusion of spices and flavours that enticed the group to partake in the culinary feast.

As they settled into their seats, William inquired about Soo Ah's whereabouts. "Where's Soo Ah?" he asked Jun Hyuk, who occupied a seat next to Hugh.

Jun Hyuk's face brightened as he spotted his wife approaching. "Ah, here she is," he exclaimed as Soo Ah joined them. In a friendly gesture, she tried to hand Daniela her forgotten lip gloss and a pill she left behind in the lobby's bathroom, prompting Hugh to playfully intervene and get hold of both items.

"Looks like someone left their glamour behind," Hugh teased, examining the lip gloss before passing it to Daniela. The playful banter took an unexpected turn when Daniela, with a touch of rudeness, snatched only the lip gloss from Hugh's hand and briskly walked away to the buffet. Hugh, intentionally leading Daniela's attention away from the pill, examined the pill and put it in his pocket.

"What a rude brat," Hugh muttered under his breath, a hint of irritation in his tone.

Soo Ah, attempting to defuse the tension, leaned towards Hugh and whispered, "Don't take it too seriously. I suppose this is how your child behaves when you've promised them all your wealth," hoping to keep the comment discreet from the Hottingers.

"It's a shame about Yahia," Mrs Hottinger began. "Such a tragedy. I do hope the police find the person responsible soon."

The sentiment was shared around the table, each member expressing their concern for Yahia's untimely death.

"I'm curious to know what the police have uncovered so far," Jake inquired.

"Nothing substantial," Hugh lied, attempting to quell any burgeoning interest Jake might have in the murder mystery.

"It's disheartening that such a dark cloud looms over what was supposed to be a memorable trip. But let's not let it overshadow the beautiful moments we've shared here," Mike added.

"Yes! Despite the unfortunate events, I'll treasure the memories of our time here. The ancient history, the vibrant markets—it's been a cultural immersion." Jaqueline said while enjoying a cup of Egyptian tea.

Mr Hottinger nodded, "I agree. Egypt has a way of leaving a lasting impression. I'm glad we could share this experience, despite the challenges."

The conversation shifted to lighter topics, with Jun Hyuk praising the Egyptian cuisine. "I must say, the food here is exquisite. The spices, the textures—it's a culinary adventure I'll remember."

Jake chimed in, "Absolutely. I never thought I'd enjoy Egyptian food so much. The flavours are so distinct and rich."

Plates of *koshari*, falafel, and stuffed grape leaves filled the table as the group enthusiastically delved into their dinner. Brigitte, savouring a bite of *koshari*, remarked, "I'll miss these authentic Egyptian dishes. It's a taste of this beautiful country we'll carry with us."

Daniela entered the terrace, gracefully balancing a substantial plate of *feteer meshaltet* meant for the entire group.

"Here, Ethan, William, try some," Mike offered, passing over a plate. The aroma of the delicacy wafted through the air, enticing the group with its tempting fragrance.

Hugh seized a plate of the dip traditionally paired with *feteer meshaltet*, a delightful blend of molasses and tahini. Unable to resist, he indulged in the rich flavours of his *feteer*.

"Did you know they used to offer these to the Gods in ancient Egyptian temples?" Mrs Hottinger shared with a chuckle, adding a touch of cultural context to the culinary experience.

As they savoured the dish, Jun Hyuk expressed his sentiment. "I will miss this, everyone," he said, capturing the moment with his camera.

"Ethan, you're quite the photographer. Look at the pictures you took in Sinai," Jun Hyuk remarked, showing Hugh the camera, and swiping through the photos.

Hugh examined the images and modestly responded, "I don't think I'm that good of a photographer," hinting the criticism towards Ethan.

"Come on, let's get together for one last photo," Jun Hyuk suggested.

"But this time, without Yahia..." Jacqueline remarked with a tinge of sadness.

"Oh dear..." Mrs Hottinger said.

"Let me capture it. I'm not particularly fond of being in pictures," Hugh volunteered.

"But it's for the memory; you should be in it too," Soo Ah insisted.

"I'm sure you'll all remember me without a photo," Hugh quipped, boosting his ego.

The group huddled closely together, ready to capture the moment in a photograph.

"Say cheese," William prompted, inviting the group to pose.

The flash flickered, and Hugh scrutinized the photo he had taken. "I think my skills are better than Ethan's," he muttered under his breath. As he deeply examined the image, a sudden realisation struck him. He swiped back to the photo Ethan had taken during their first dinner in Sinai before Yahia's murder.

Hugh whispered to William, "I've found the murder weapon."

"What? What is it?" William asked urgently.

Hugh noticed Brigitte surveying the gathering within the confined space, her eyes traversing the assorted faces amidst the indoor throng. The ambient buzz of conversation echoed, blending with the muted clinking of cutlery and the occasional laughter that punctuated the air.

Sensing a momentary escape, Brigitte deftly retrieved her room keys from the table, fingers closing around the cool metal. An undercurrent of nervousness marked her demeanour, subtly betraying an unease that lingered beneath the composed façade she presented to the casual observer.

With a sidelong glance towards the bustling crowd, she excused herself, a hint of apprehension tinging her voice.

"I'll head to the bathroom," she uttered, her words carrying a subtle urgency that betrayed the disquiet simmering beneath the surface.

"She grabbed her room keys; she must be heading over to her room," Hugh said as he rose to follow her. "I need to get in there, one last piece of the puzzle is missing."

"How are you going to enter her room?" William whispered impatiently.

"I know how. Try to distract her; I need fifteen minutes," Hugh whispered. "Oh and prepare a room where everyone is gathered; ask Detective Salah to bring in Chef Fakhri and Mohammed. Everyone needs to be there."

"Must it always be a big reveal?"

"Always."

## CHAPTER 16: WINDOW VIEW

The crisp night air wrapped around Hugh as he slipped out of the Cleo Hotel, his steps masked by the rhythmic hum of the city. The moon cast an ethereal glow on the imposing structure as he scanned the exterior for a covert ascent to the third floor. With cat-like agility, he navigated the fire escape, each rung a silent accomplice in his clandestine venture.

"Oh, dear lord," he muttered, glancing down below. "Ethan, you're missing all the fun."

Upon reaching the third floor, Hugh surveyed the array of windows, his determination unwavering as he sought the one harbouring Brigitte's concealed secrets. The exterior of the Cleo Hotel, a mosaic of architectural nuances, posed both challenge and opportunity. His fingers delicately grazed the cool surface of the windowsills, seeking the subtle imprints that hinted at familiarity.

As Hugh endeavoured to identify Brigitte's sanctuary, the moonlight became a shroud, veiling the details of the building's façade. Undeterred, he relied on his intuition, choosing a window that whispered promises of revelation.

"This appears to be room 305," Hugh mused, his voice carrying a hint of uncertainty.

With a calculated effort, Hugh eased open the chosen window and slipped into the room beyond. However, instead of the anticipated encounter with Brigitte, he found himself in the dimly lit abode of an elderly man, his room adorned with relics of a bygone era.

Time seemed to hang in the air as Hugh processed the unintended intrusion. The old man stirred in his sleep, moulding a disoriented gaze towards the unexpected visitor. In the tense silence, Hugh grappled with the urgency to retreat unnoticed.

"Who's there?" the old man said.

"Oh no," Hugh murmured under his breath.

As the room's occupant roused further, Hugh, like a phantom, made a swift decision. He edged towards the window, his escape route hinging on agility and discretion.

With practised finesse, Hugh slipped through the window, returning to the nocturnal embrace of the exterior. The night air crackled with anticipation as he manoeuvred along the ledge, his destination fixed on the window adjacent to the old man's room—the window concealing Brigitte's enigmatic presence.

In a heartbeat, he found himself balancing on the narrow precipice, the cityscape below a distant mosaic of lights.

"Well, it appears my instincts can falter at times. *This* must be room 305."

As Hugh approached Brigitte's window, he caught glimpses of her silhouette within. The window, a threshold to a web of mysteries, stood as a portal between the known and the clandestine. With his breath held, he reached for the window latch.

"Here we go."

Hugh stealthily entered the room through the window, the fabric of the curtain a soft rustle as it enveloped him like an undercover accomplice. The room was dimly lit, embellished with the flickering glow of a single bedside lamp.

Cocooned behind the curtain, Hugh surveyed the room, his senses heightened by the palpable anticipation. He could hear hushed voices, the cadence of which sent ripples through the charged atmosphere.

As the curtain veiled him from their view, Hugh identified one figure in the room. Brigitte, with an air of mystery cloaked around her, stood in conversation with a man obscured in the shadows. The silhouette hinted at familiarity.

"Why have you come here? The police are skulking about, and, joy of joys, I am graced with two detectives within our tour group. What a stroke of luck!" Brigitte confronted the shadowy figure, her eyes widened with unease.

"I'm boarding a boat to Italy tonight, making my way to Paris from there. The boss will meet with me, and I'll hand this over." Hugh discerned the man's gesture towards his bag, its contents remaining an enigma.

"Why risk it, then?"

The voice, cutting and accusatory, shattered the quiet. "I came to ask one question. Brigitte, you can't escape the truth. It was you, wasn't it?"

"I've done nothing! What on earth are you talking about?" Brigitte countered.

"Yahia's blood is on your hands. You murdered him."

"No! That's absurd. I loved Yahia. Why would I harm him?"

The man sneered, his voice cutting through the tense air. "Loved him? Don't play innocent. I've seen the darkness within you."

As Brigitte staunchly denied any involvement, the man persisted, accusing her of Yahia's death. "You've been living a lie, Brigitte. Pretending to be something you're not."

"Like you haven't been living a lie? You have been hiding your true self. In fact, you're even more deceptive than I am. Now, leave before someone catches sight of you."

In the shadows, Hugh could only see a sinister smile played across the man's face as he spoke, "The authorities won't find me. I'm here to unveil the truth, to expose the murderer you've become."

Yassine, Yahia's estranged brother, emerged from the shadows like a ghost from the past. Hugh, concealed behind the curtain, grappled with the surge of emotions that threatened to betray his stoic façade.

"Yassine, for a moment there, I thought you were Yahia," Hugh remarked sarcastically, emerging from his hiding spot.

"Who are you?" Yassine shouted aggressively.

"Ethan?" Brigitte gasped; her face drained of colour.

"Let's just say I'm the person who'll hand you over to the authorities," Hugh replied calmly as he approached Yassine.

"Why... why did you follow me? Was this why William was trying to distract me on my way here?" Brigitte questioned, her hands rising to rest atop her head in confusion.

The air crackled with tension as Hugh and Yassine faced each other. Yassine seized a vase from the coffee table and hurled it towards Hugh, who deftly evaded it.

Without a word, Yassine threw a fist blow that Hugh narrowly dodged. The room echoed with the impact, a precursor to the impending brawl. Yassine, fuelled by pent-up frustration, lunged forward with a series of rapid jabs, each punch aimed at Hugh's defences.

"You're not escaping; it's too late now," Hugh declared, wiping blood from his face with his thumb.

"You Brits always like deciding for others, don't you?" Yassine sneered sinisterly.

"Yassine, stop!" Brigitte, caught in the crossfire, tried to intervene. Her pleas were drowned out by the tumult of the scuffle. Desperately, she extended her hands in a futile attempt to separate the combatants, but the chaotic conflict seemed beyond her control.

Yassine, driven by a relentless desire to prove himself, launched a powerful kick that grazed Hugh's side. The sharp pain intensified Hugh's determination, and he retaliated with a swift, well-aimed counter, connecting with Yassine's shoulder.

As the final blows were exchanged, both men stood panting, their bodies marked by the physical toll of the confrontation. The shadows, still and heavy, seemed to absorb the echoes of their silent struggle, leaving behind an aftermath of bruised egos.

With a final jab, Yassine managed to bring Hugh to the ground, continuing to throw fists that Hugh desperately tried to evade.

Just as the confrontation reached its peak, the door burst open, and William stormed into the room. With a swift and decisive move, he restrained Yassine, his strength quelling the storm of aggression.

"Dr Harrington, finally making an appearance," Hugh quipped sarcastically.

"Is this enough to convince you to stop doing this solo?" William gestured as he held Yassine tightly.

Hugh, now battered and bruised, lay on the floor, his breath ragged, yet determination etched across his features. Through swollen eyes, he managed a smile.

"What's that in your hand?" Hugh inquired, breathless.

"The lab report of the pills, Detective Salah handed it over to me," William replied, passing the report to Hugh as he continued putting all his force in restraining Yassine. As Hugh scanned the report with his eyes, his breath came heavily.

"I was right," Hugh panted heavily.

"I didn't get to read it." William said.

"His bag," Hugh gasped, attempting to rise from the floor.

Recognizing the gravity of the situation, William opened the bag as instructed. A gasp escaped him.

"The missing Ankh from the Egyptian museum..." William uttered.

The Ankh gleamed in the darkness. Hugh, battered but resolute, locked eyes with William—a silent acknowledgment of the significance of their discovery.

## CHAPTER 17: THE MURDERER

Detective Salah extended his arm theatrically, indicating the assembled tour group and Sunrise Inn staff.

"Everyone's present," he remarked, gesturing towards Yassine, who sat quietly, an enigma amidst the crowd. "They were perplexed by the resemblance," he explained, "but I clarified that he's the twin. Mohammed, on the other hand, seemed disappointed to see him."

Mohammed took a seat, his gaze fixed on Yassine. Spotting Ethan and William, he eagerly waved, and William reciprocated the gesture.

"What did he uncover?" Detective Salah inquired of William, gesturing towards Hugh. Hugh's once-neat hair was now tousled, and the white shirt he wore was dishevelled from its usual place within the confines of his black trousers, courtesy of the altercation with Yassine.

"He has all the relevant details; he's about to divulge everything," William replied, and Hugh, catching a hint of scepticism in Detective Salah's tone about the grand venue choice, heard William chuckle. "Ethan enjoys a touch of extravagance. Sit back and relish the spectacle," William remarked, making Hugh smile at the familiar understanding between them.

The ballroom at Cleo Hotel was decorated with opulent Egyptian tapestries and bathed in a warm golden glow and regal elegance. The polished marble floor and ceiling adorned with intricate chandeliers cast a soft illumination upon the group.

"What's going on?" Derek asked impatiently, glancing between the three men.

Hugh strategically positioned himself at the centre of the room, recognizing that power secured the best vantage point. To quell the growing murmur, he rhythmically tapped his water bottle on the table.

"We've identified Yahia's murderer," he announced, commanding the attention of the assembled group.

Yassine, unable to contain his agitation, attempted to rise but was restrained by Brigitte, who firmly gripped his arm.

"Don't touch me." Yassine shoved Brigitte's hand off his arms.

"You!" Detective Salah snapped sharply, silencing any potential outburst.

"How could someone among us do something so terrible?" Soo-Ah nervously murmured, finding solace in her husband's comforting embrace.

"It will be over soon, Soo Ah, don't worry," Jun Hyuk reassured her.

"Oh, finally, the poor man can rest in peace," Mr Hottinger remarked.

Hugh's cold tone cut through the air as he addressed Yassine, who felt his face flush red.

"After three months at Sinai Bird Agency, you decided that change wasn't for you. The pay was low, and you had grander dreams, right?"

Yassine shifted uncomfortably as the accusations mounted. Hugh continued, revealing the intricate dynamics between the brothers.

"You desired to depart your homeland and proposed that Yahia take your position there. Yahia excelled as an employee, unlike yourself, which clarifies Yahia's altered behaviour in the travel agency. However, your unfortunate brother, who relinquished his identity for your sake, remained in the shadows. He was unaware that you were still treading this path, or worse, descending into a darker one. The evidence lies within Yahia's journal; he truly cared for you, you know? What a regrettable situation."

"Even if I've betrayed my country, I'd never harm my brother!" Yassine nervously protested, defending himself against the weighty accusations.

"After resigning as a tour guide, you persisted on the deceitful path, journeying to Paris for a lucrative yet unethical trade, accompanied by none other than Brigitte."

"I… I…" Brigitte stammered.

"Was your apology letter to Yahia nothing but a web of lies? Were your remorseful words genuine, Brigitte?" Hugh inquired.

"Brig, what... What's going on?" Jacqueline stuttered, yet Brigitte remained silent, maintaining eye contact with her best friend.

"Sometimes you believe you know someone, only to realise you don't know them at all," Hugh remarked icily to Jacqueline.

"You're caught red-handed. Both of you," Hugh declared, producing the Ankh from Yassine's possession. "The missing Ankh from the Egyptian Museum."

"Oh, my word…" Detective Salah exclaimed. "I can't believe this…" He hurried over to Hugh and took hold of the artifact.

"Listen, there's no escaping this now," Hugh asserted, his tone unwavering. Yassine's face flushed with the realisation of the gravity of his actions, the betrayal of his country looming over him like an impending storm.

"Brig... What is all this? Tell me! What's going on? Is this why you suggested we come to Egypt? What's happening?" Jacqueline demanded, a mixture of confusion and concern etched across her face.

"I... I'm so sorry," Brigitte stammered, tears welling up in her eyes.

"If you're genuinely remorseful, enlighten us on how the Ankh ended up with the two of you. Perhaps your punishment will be more lenient," Detective Salah exclaimed.

"I... I work with the Louvre Paris, but there's a group within the institution that the management doesn't know about, dealing with stolen antiques. We produce replicas and substitute the originals with them, operating within the black market of antiques. Through this shadow network, I got acquainted with Yassine, as they engage with illicit antique dealers here in Egypt. Yassine's internship was organized to finalize the plan of introducing the replica into Egypt and the Ankh heist. It's way more extensive than the two of us; we're merely assisting higher-ups in the operation." Brigitte wiped away her tears as she glanced at Jacqueline and continued, "I developed a close bond with Yahia during his brother's internship. I secretly hoped for our relationship to evolve into something more. Two days before Yahia and Yassine returned to Egypt, Yahia unexpectedly visited my office at the Louvre. The door was slightly open, and he overheard our conversation."

"Yes, he had seen both of us… She was showing me the first draft of the Ankh, talking about the details of replacing the original. We were deciding on when she would come to Egypt to deliver the replica, allowing the others here to execute the heist," Yassine explained.

Brigitte nodded.

"At that moment, he entered the office, and I could sense Yahia's heartbeat accelerating, mirroring the pace of my own. Yahia pointed accusingly at the counterfeit Ankh resting on the desk beside me. I… I tried to return it to its box. He questioned Yassine about how he could do such a thing, his mind clearly in panic. I think he never expected that his brother would take things to such extremes. I assured him I could explain, but he wouldn't look at me. The pain cut deep; he couldn't bring himself to meet my gaze and I felt shame and disappointment. Yahia was the last person I wanted to discover my true identity. Then… then he slowly turned to look at me. I wish he never did because that moment was agonizing. I recognized the courage it took for him to meet my eyes and he said, 'We may not have known each other long, but I thought you were someone else entirely.'"

"And that's when you penned him the apology letter and presented him with the leather bag," Hugh articulated. "Yes..."
"But it was all a lie, wasn't it? On the day of his murder, when we were all gathered to hear Yahia's instructions, something tumbled out of his bag. Recall that discussion while we were watching the news report, Mrs Hottinger?" He turned to Mrs Hottinger, who nodded impatiently. "You were right; it was an Ankh."

"Hey, I guessed that one right, too," Jake interjected.

"Your leather bag is impeccably maintained compared to Yahia's. It wasn't his bag; the Ankh fell out of your bag—it was yours. Wrapped up with your best friend's handkerchief. You must've unknowingly swapped your bag with Yahia's. He knew you lied again, and that's when Daniela witnessed the both of you arguing in your room after check-in. He seemed very absent-minded during dinner. You lied to him again," Hugh articulated.

"I did... but I swear this time, my sincerity was genuine. I had handed the replica to Yahia, telling him my desire to exit the illicit trade. That act served as my guarantee, entrusting it back to him. I let him know of my intention to meet Yassine at midnight at the inn and pass it on to him. Yahia told me to ask Yassine to rendezvous with him at the mountain's edge, their customary spot for discussions. Yassine arrived at our room in the inn shrouded in the quiet of the night while Jaq was in the study room and everyone else slept. I told him that Yahia waited him by the mountain," Brigitte disclosed.

"So, the person I witnessed fleeing was you!" Jake exclaimed, his gaze directed accusingly at Yassine.

"You devil! You've killed your own brother!" Mrs Hottinger's voice rang out, echoed by Mr Hottinger, who branded him a betrayer.

"I find it hard to believe that you would do such a thing, Yassine. Yahia cherished you more than anything. He dedicated his entire life to you," Mohammed expressed, his tone laced with disappointment and a sense of disbelief.

A chorus of accusations erupted from the others, casting blame upon Yassine and Brigitte with fervour.

"Hey, hey, everyone, let's try to calm down," Mike suggested, his voice seeking to restore a semblance of tranquillity to the heated atmosphere.

"I did not murder my brother!" Yassine retorted, his voice rising above the cacophony of accusations. "Maybe she did!" he pointed at Brigitte who was still in tears.

"Look," Hugh interjected emphatically, striding purposefully around the room, a water bottle clasped in one hand while the other nestled in his pocket. He positioned himself behind Yassine, who steadfastly refused to turn and face him. "We discovered the handkerchief in the market, and eyewitnesses claim they saw you there after the murder. What were you doing there?"

"It was where I met Brigitte to discuss the next step. But she still wanted out. We talked about the details of Yahia's murder, but her friend, the blonde here, interrupted us, and I had to leave. But something inside me told me that she might be the one who murdered him. I wanted to uncover the truth, so I went searching for her near the travel agency, hoping she'd claim her refund—our agency's policy, refunding tourists for any unforeseen circumstances. Unfortunately, she didn't turn up, leaving me no choice but to pay her a visit here, at the Cleo Hotel," Yassine explained.

"It was him—the man you were conversing with in the market," Jacqueline concluded.

Brigitte pressed her lips together, nodding with tears in her eyes.

"No remorse whatsoever; your brother is dead, and you still proceed with the heist, hmm," Hugh tutted.

"Listen to me! I did not murder my brother," Yassine asserted firmly.

"You most certainly did," Hugh asserted more firmly.

"I... I did go to the mountain edge, but he was already dead! I yelled in panic as I came across my brother's lifeless body on the ground. I... I turned the body only to see my brother's face with a half-smile. I was in shock, then I... I heard someone nearing and, without thinking, I grabbed the Ankh replica from his bag and fled. I stood far away, away from prying eyes, disbelieving, crying uncontrollably, but you wouldn't know that!" Yassine sarcastically smiled, his eyes moist but holding back tears. "I am telling you; it wasn't me who murdered him."

"You believed you could escape the country after swapping the Ankh and exploiting your brother?!" Detective Salah exclaimed with his typical aggression. "You and those involved will rot in jail."

The Korean couple cast a disappointed glance at Yassine and Brigitte as Detective Salah secured Yassine and Brigitte with handcuffs.

"I... I'm so sorry..." Brigitte uttered.

"Wow... He's your brother," Derek rebuked Yassine.

"I've had quite the time here in Egypt," Hugh quipped sarcastically.

"So, who's responsible for Yahia's murder? Did they do it?" Jake inquired, his impatience evident in his tone.

Hugh surveyed the room, observing the varied reactions, yet paid no heed to them. His discerning gaze traversed each person before settling on Chef Fakhri.

"The murderer trailed Yahia to the mountain and callously ended his life. Regrettably, you bore witness to the killer while tending to the charcoal outside the hotel," Hugh implicated the elderly chef.

"What are you implying? I have nothing to do with Yahia's murder! I didn't see anyone either," Chef Fakhri retorted, his voice escalating.

"If you didn't see the murderer on the day of the murder, then what did you see? One thing I know for sure is that the murderer manipulated you adeptly. Using that ring, thinking it could secure your son's affections. What other promises did they make to you?" Hugh accused.

"Daniela?" Detective Salah exclaimed.

"Me? What do you mean?" Daniela responded, her expression one of perplexity.

"I… I…" Chef Fakhri stammered.

"Take your time; I'll get back to you," Hugh echoed, behaving rather childishly.

Hugh approached Mr Hottinger, requesting permission to examine the cane. Once granted, he delicately opened the red-plated palm grip handle, revealing a gold eagle beak underneath. Strikingly, the eagle was missing both of its eyes.

"Does it open?" Jun Hyuk murmured to Soo Ah, his words audible to everyone present.

"Wow, a gold-plated eagle beak missing a little of its paint. But don't worry, we've found it, inside Yahia's brain," Hugh exclaimed, genuinely surprised to see the eagle beak.

"That's awful...." Derek said.

"It is..." Mike agreed.

"Why are the eyes missing, Mr Hottinger? Also, I am quite surprised that someone as affluent as you are using a cane made of rather inexpensive materials," Hugh inquired.

"I... I don't know... and, of course, I would use something more economical while travelling. I don't want to draw too much attention to myself," he stuttered, visibly perturbed by the unexpected revelation. "I wasn't involved in his murder!"

"One faux black crystal was discovered on a path close to the crime scene, making your cane, Mr Hottinger, emerge as the murder weapon. A blunt force hit in the front with no sharp edge and a blow on the back of the head with a sharp edge—the top of your cane—causing instant death. The second faux black crystal was found in the shared bathroom in the lobby.

Unable to locate the other crystal, the murderer disposed of it in the sink, down the drain, just like that," Hugh declared calmly, elegantly swinging Mr Hottinger's cane through the air.

"The murderer did attempt to conceal all traces, but I suppose their efforts weren't quite astute enough. The photos on Jun Hyuk's camera lay bare everything. In a picture Ethan—I mean… I—captured before Yahia's murder, Mr Hottinger's red-plated palm grip handle failed to shine. However, in the photo we took today, parts of the handle were gleaming uniformly under the flash. Why? Because part of it had been painted in rather an interesting way."

Hugh approached Mrs Hottinger and held her hand. "Painted with your metallic red nail polish," Hugh elucidated as he meticulously peeled off the painted layers on the cane.

"This... this is ridiculous!" Mrs Hottinger protested; her voice strained with disbelief.

"What are you talking about?" Mr Hottinger shouted in disbelief.

Hugh retrieved Daniela's pill and the medical report, acquired during and after dinner, from his pocket.

"Daniela, these pills of yours, they're not anxiety medication. They're opioids, a narcotic pain medication. Even for short-term use, they can cause addiction. These pills aren't providing you relief; they're fuelling your substance use," Hugh disclosed.

"What on earth are you talking about? You must be out of your mind!" Mrs Hottinger retorted.

"This is preposterous, Ethan. The doctor is Flavia's friend since high school, and we know him very well," Mr Hottinger added with frustration.

"Thank you for the information," Hugh acknowledged. "It further strengthens the belief that Mrs Hottinger was well aware of her friend, the doctor, and his prescriptions."

The whole room gasped.

"Are you out of your mind?" Mr Hottinger retorted.

"My aunt would never do something like that," Daniela exclaimed.

"He's undoubtedly lost his sanity," Mrs Hottinger interjected.

"Mrs Hottinger, if anyone is displaying signs of madness, it would be you for deceiving your own brother and niece," Hugh said, locking eyes with her. He handed the medical report to Mr Hottinger.

"Flavia…" Mr Hottinger said in shock.

"Why… Aunt Flavia… Why?" Daniela spoke slowly, addressing her aunt.

"Why? Because your father promised all his wealth to you, and only you. Nothing for his sister," Hugh stated coldly.

"Yahia had overheard something he shouldn't have. Let's just say, he interfered in someone else's affairs. He was captured on CCTV before we headed to Sinai, engaged in an altercation with someone. It appeared to be a heated argument about certain pills," Hugh explained as he retrieved the black tassel and approached Mrs Hottinger, who was draped in her brown shawl. "The culprit behind Yahia's murder is none other than Mrs Hottinger," Hugh declared, aligning the black tassel with the vacant space in Mrs Hottinger's shawl.

A collective gasp swept through the room, prompting an enraged outburst from Yassine, who Detective Salah struggled to restrain.

"I've been saying it's not me!" Yassine shouted.

"You've extinguished every ounce of love and trust he had in you by betraying him once more," Hugh retorted sarcastically to Yassine.

Mrs Hottinger, seemingly taken aback, exclaimed, "This... this is ridiculous. Nico, Daniela, don't believe him."

"One question for you, Mr Hottinger, did you grant permission for Chef Fakhri to retain the ring, a cherished heirloom in your family?" Hugh inquired. "He claimed to have discussed it with the Hottingers, and you supposedly agreed to let him keep it."

"The... the ring? You've found the ring?" Mr Hottinger responded with a perplexed question.

"I guess he spoke to only one Hottinger." Hugh half smiled and continued, "Are you still in denial?" Hugh inquired, staring at Mrs Hottinger. He then redirected his gaze towards Chef Fakhri.

"Chef Fakhri, you deceived us, didn't you? It was Mrs Hottinger whom you witnessed that night, not Daniela. She was the one who gave you the ring in return for your silence. Lies, lies, lies."

"I promise you, Detective Ethan, I am as surprised as everyone else. I had no idea she was the murderer. Yes, I lied. I did not see anyone that night while tending to the charcoal. But on the day of Yahia's murder, just before dinner, I saw a heated argument between Mrs Hottinger and Yahia, although I wasn't quite sure about the details. After the murder occurred, before you began questioning me, Mrs Hottinger asked me not to mention anything, fearing everyone would think she was the murderer. I believed her. Despite my initial resistance, she persuaded me with the ring, claiming it was all she had. Blinded by desperation, I accepted it. I never imagined she would go so far as to murder Yahia. I would've never accepted if I had known…" Chef Fakhri explained sincerely.

"Why did you falsely claim it was Daniela then?" Hugh inquired.

"During the football game, Mrs Hottinger approached me. She mentioned her brother had noticed, and she needed to create a distraction. She assured me that she would handle it discreetly, allowing her brother and niece to forget about the incident. Concerned about potential police involvement, I asked what I should say if the authorities discovered the ring in my possession."

"Mrs Hottinger advised me to claim it was Daniela who gave it to me and assured me she could manipulate the situation. She emphasised Daniela's age, expressing confidence that she could convince everyone she had given me the ring. Mrs Hottinger promised I could keep the ring and pledged to send me money once she returned to Switzerland. I saw it as an opportunity for my… my daughters," Chef Fakhri confessed.

"Very foolish to place your trust in that, and certainly disappointing for your children," Hugh remarked.

"Flavia, please, is this all true?" Mr Hottinger implored.

"Tell them, Mrs. Hottinger. Let them know. It's too late now, and there's no way out," Hugh said.

"You can't believe him dear...." Mrs. Hottinger said.

"Like Detective Ethan said, there's no way out Mrs. Hottinger. Admitting now might give you some leniency." Detective Salah pressed.

Mrs Hottinger remained quiet for a moment until she finally cracked under the accusing eyes focused on her.

"It's all your fault." She locked eyes with her brother with teary eyes and fists clenched. "Your only sister, left with no one by her side, and you leave her nothing of your wealth. How could you do to me exactly what my late husband did to me? You've fuelled my hatred, bred resentment. You've pushed away everyone and made my animosity unstoppable."

"Aunt Flavia..." Daniela said.

"No more Aunt Flavia, Daniela. I was never on your side," Mrs Hottinger said. She shifted her gaze towards Hugh.

"I became anxious when Yahia overheard my conversation with the doctor friend in Switzerland. He discovered that the pills I was providing Daniela weren't actual anxiety medication; that they were the real cause of her addiction. He confronted me, and I attempted to deny it but eventually admitted that I would make her stop. The day before we went to Sinai, he had seen the pills with Daniela again and confronted me for a second time. I suppose this is where you caught me on CCTV. The last confrontation was in Sinai after he saw the pills with Daniela once more. That fool should've stayed out of it!" Mrs Hottinger disclosed.

"Things escalated when Yahia threatened to inform Nico first thing in the morning. At our first dinner in Saint Catherine, I attempted to convey that I had stopped providing Daniela with the medications. But Yahia seemed preoccupied and distracted. and I couldn't stay put; I knew that if my brother found out, I might lose my inheritance plans."

"He was preoccupied thinking about the Ankh, not Daniela's medication…" William said.

"My plan was to inherit all my brother's fortune by turning Daniela into an addict, then sending her to rehab or jail, was falling apart. I refused to let someone like a tour guide we had met just a little more than two weeks ago ruin my plans. That night, I followed Yahia while Nico slept and took his cane. When I reached Yahia, I struck him twice. First, I hit him on the face with the bottom of the cane, then flipped it to the sharp end, the eagle beak, and struck him on the back of his head. I went back to the inn through a secluded area so no one could see me. I was afraid; I was scared of losing my reputation this way," Mrs Hottinger confessed, her voice trembling.

"Certainly, reputation takes precedence over family and a tour guide, without a doubt," Hugh remarked sarcastically.

"I... I..." Chef Fakhri began, his voice filled with regret. "I'm so sorry, young lady," he said, addressing Daniela, as he sank into his chair, remorseful.

The Korean couple and the three architects offered solace to Mr Hottinger and his daughter.

"Let's go, Mrs Hottinger," Detective Salah said as he approached her, cuffing her delicate wrists adorned with jewellery.

"I need an embassy representative," she demanded.

"We can continue this conversation at the police station," Detective Salah responded. "Time to move, both of you," Detective Salah said, extending assistance to Yassine and Brigitte as they rose from their chairs, their wrists now restrained. As he steered the trio towards the ballroom exit, Detective Salah approached Hugh and whispered, "Appreciate your help, my friend. I owe you a grand dinner once my promotion comes through. Only thing left for me is to find the White Masked Killer."

"Good luck." William said.

Hugh stood next to William as they watched Detective Salah take the criminals away.

"That was rather intense, a lot of probing," William commented. "How did you know the cane opens?"

"It struck me while we were signing the forms in the travel agency. Air bubbles emerging from the pen reminded me of the excruciating sound coming from Mr Hottinger's cane. Air bubbles cracking from his cane mean only one thing: there's an opening."

"Excruciating? What an exaggerated choice of word," William said.

"The eagle beak, though? That was just me hoping I was right." A blend of relief and heaviness settled in Hugh's heart, and a throbbing headache struck him.

"Heading out already?" William asked, gripping him firmly as he anticipated Ethan's return.

"No, not yet" Hugh whispered, resisting Ethan's comeback. "Let's go to the falafel joint from Ethan's memory."

"One last meal, eh?" William teased.

"Hey, lad, up for some falafel?" Hugh inquired of the distressed teenager, Mohammed.

"Always up for *taamiyya*," Mohammed smiled.

"Go on, I'll catch up shortly. There's one final matter I need to attend to," William declared, striding purposefully towards Mike.

Hugh grinned, well aware of William's intentions.

## **CHAPTER 18: ETHAN, HUGH, AND …**

"I just got off the phone with Detective Salah. Even though he did not solve the case of the White Masked Killer, he still got the promotion, Head of Homicide Department," William remarked, settling beside Ethan in the living room that overlooked the garden to Ethan's London house. Ethan was engrossed in playing games on his Atari, quite distracted.

"It's good to be back home, isn't it?" William asked. "The harsh chill of London's weather is settling in."

"I went on a trip to Egypt, but it felt like I wasn't really there. Hugh had to show up, spoil my holiday and give me a few bruises all over my face," Ethan grumbled, still glued to his Atari 5200. "Looking forward to our trip to Russia next week, though!"

"Didn't you say you'd prepare that recipe from the *taamiyya* joint's owner?"

"At the moment, William, I could use a break from *taamiyya*. Hugh overindulged me with it, and he succeeded in turning my cravings off. I need some time away to rekindle my appetite for it," Ethan remarked, still engrossed in his game.

William chuckled, understanding Ethan's sentiments. Being physically present yet not truly present could indeed be perplexing. Since the Sinai mystery had been resolved, Hugh hadn't made a single appearance.

"Argh! I lost again," Ethan exclaimed, flinging the joystick controller onto the table before him. He stood, yawned, and stretched. "I'll go get the mail. Let's see what bills are waiting for me this month."

Heading to the mailbox by the gate, Ethan sifted through the letters. Among them, one letter caught his eye. He opened it and his expression changed dramatically. Ethan stared intently at the contents of the letter.

*Dear Ethan,*

*Summon the fortitude within you and embark on the quest to locate me.*

*Warm regards,*

*The elusive individual you seek*

"Stamped with the address 'Royal Gardens, Kensington Heights, London SW1'. Why is my parents' house address stamped at the back?"

Suddenly, a sharp pain shot through his head, causing him to wince and clutch his temples tightly, falling to his knees.

"Any special bills for me? I practically live with you, you know," William's light-hearted jest drifted in from the garden. However, upon seeing Ethan on his knees, he rushed to his side.

"Ethan? Let me help you," William offered, but Ethan remained still. His grip on William's arm tightened, and he turned to face him, their eyes locking in a moment of shared concern.

"Good day, Son."

******

**Fall 1964**

The plump eleven-year-old boy sat quietly at his desk. The bell rang, signalling the end of math class and the imminent arrival of the history teacher.

"Hey, Wayne, have you revised for this test?" Ethan asked.

"Of course I have!" Wayne, with his soft blonde hair and glasses that covered much of his face, replied arrogantly,

The history teacher entered just as Wayne boasted.

"Alright, class, I'll start handing out your test papers," she said softly, met with the enthusiastic response of the sixth graders.

Ethan felt nervous as he awaited his test paper. He hadn't put in any effort to study and found the paper incredibly challenging to comprehend. In desperation, he whispered to Wayne, who had been scribbling away since the start.

"Wayne... Wayne, can you help me with question 4A?"

Ignoring him, Wayne kept writing. But Ethan persisted, whispering again, "Come on, Wayne, if you don't show me your test paper right now, I'll eat your lunch!"

"Why would you do that?" Wayne whispered back, confused. "You've already got yours!"

Ms. Lawlor, with her short temper, overheard their conversation. "Ethan! Wayne! Bring your test papers here this instant!" she yelled, reprimanding them for their chat.

Later that afternoon, both children's parents were called in and informed about the incident. Ethan's parents scolded him on the way home, and his father was particularly upset with the teacher's words.

"Go wash up upstairs; there's no cake for you today," Ethan's mother scolded as soon as they arrived home. Her beautiful dark brown eyes matched her son's, but Ethan took after his father with his dull, dark brown hair, failing to inherit her silky light brown locks.

It was already evening, and Ethan was in his room. He'd had dinner but wasn't allowed his favourite cakes. A knock on the door startled him. "Is it Dad? Has he come to scold me again?"

"Ethan, my dear boy, care to join me downstairs in my study for some cake?" peeked his grandfather through the door.

"Grandpa!" Ethan exclaimed happily.

"It's always better to share a carrot cake," his grandfather said playfully, winking.

In the study room, Ethan devoured the carrot cake as if he'd been starving for days, despite being a food-loving chubby boy.

"So, what happened in school today?" his grandfather asked after Ethan finished his cake.

"To be honest, Grandpa, I didn't study for my history test, and I asked Wayne if I could copy his answers, but he said no," Ethan admitted honestly, feeling unafraid as his grandfather was always understanding. Ethan had never seen his grandpa lose his temper, which made him feel safe being truthful.

"That wasn't very kind of you, Ethan," his grandfather said, settling into his rocking chair. "Wayne got scolded for no reason, and he'd studied hard for that test."

Ethan felt ashamed and remained silent.

"Tomorrow, you should apologise to Wayne and your teacher. You need to take responsibility for your mistakes," his grandfather advised.

"But Grandpa..." Ethan's voice trembled, "I'd rather not. I don't think it's necessary. Maybe we could just leave it."

The old man chuckled, pulling out a beautiful round pocket watch from his pocket. "You see, Ethan, this magical pocket watch will give you courage. Here, it's yours."

Ethan rushed to his grandpa in excitement. "But this is your waistcoat watch, Grandpa! Can I really have it? Is it really magical?"

"Of course, you can, and it surely is!" laughed his grandfather.

The housemaid entered the study after a soft knock and permission from Ethan's grandfather. She placed a tray of tea on the round table.

"Shall I bring more cake, Mr Charles?"

# In the Heights of Sinai

*& the trip continues...*

In the Heights of Sinai

In the Heights of Sinai

*Written by:*
*R.Y. Adams*

In the Heights of Sinai

# In the Heights of Sinai

www.ingramcontent.com/pod-product-compliance
Lightning Source LLC
LaVergne TN
LVHW040142080526
838202LV00042B/2991